His deep voice ~~rolled over~~ the
Puget Sound.

Startled, Jolie nodded and swallowed. "Yes?"

Griff took a minute to take in the whole package.
What the heck was a beautiful woman dressed like
this doing in Harry's Diner?

"My name's Griff Price. I have a proposition for
you." He didn't miss the way her big brown eyes
widened at his choice of words.

"How do you do, Mr. Price?" Her speech was
careful and polite, her expression wary.

Sleek and sophisticated, she reminded him of
a Thoroughbred horse. Generations of carefully
chosen bloodlines came together to produce a
woman this magnificent. Good bone structure,
sleek hair, clear eyes, fine skin and good muscle
tone didn't happen by accident.

He was pretty good at sizing up women. She
didn't look like a baby-sitter.

She looked like trouble.

Dear Reader,

With summer nearly here, it's time to stock up on essentials such as sunblock, sandles and plenty of Silhouette Romance novels! Here's our checklist of page-turners to keep your days sizzling!

❏ *A Princess in Waiting* by Carol Grace (SR #1588)—In this ROYALLY WED: THE MISSING HEIR title, dashing Charles Rodin saves the day by marrying his brother's pregnant ex-wife!

❏ *Because of the Ring* by Stella Bagwell (SR #1589)—With this magical SOULMATES title, her grandmother's ring leads Claudia Westfield to the man of her dreams....

❏ *A Date with a Billionaire* by Julianna Morris (SR #1590)—Bethany Cox refused her prize—a date with the charitable Kane O'Rourke—but how can she get a gorgeous billionaire to take no for an answer? And does she really want to...?

❏ *The Marriage Clause* by Karen Rose Smith (SR #1591)—In this VIRGIN BRIDES installment, innocent Gina Foster agrees to a marriage of convenience with the wickedly handsome Clay McCormick, only to be swept into a world of passion.

❏ *The Man with the Money* by Arlene James (SR #1592)—A millionaire playboy in disguise romances a lovely foster mom. But will the truth destroy his chance at true love?

❏ *The 15 lb. Matchmaker* by Jill Limber (SR #1593)—Griff Price is the ultimate lone cowboy—until he's saddled with a baby and a jilted-bride-turned-nanny.

Be sure to come back next month for our list of great summer stories.

Happy reading!

Mary-Theresa Hussey
Senior Editor

Please address questions and book requests to:
Silhouette Reader Service
U.S.: 3010 Walden Ave., P.O. Box 1325, Buffalo, NY 14269
Canadian: P.O. Box 609, Fort Erie, Ont. L2A 5X3

The 15 lb. Matchmaker

JILL LIMBER

SILHOUETTE *Romance*

Published by Silhouette Books

America's Publisher of Contemporary Romance

To Jack—my personal hero.
I love you, forever and always.

 SILHOUETTE BOOKS

ISBN 0-373-19593-1

THE 15 LB. MATCHMAKER

Copyright © 2002 by Jill Limber

This edition published by arrangement with Harlequin Books S.A.

® and TM are trademarks of Harlequin Books S.A., used under license.
Trademarks indicated with ® are registered in the United States Patent
and Trademark Office, the Canadian Trade Marks Office and in other
countries.

Visit Silhouette at www.eHarlequin.com

Printed in U.S.A.

JILL LIMBER

lives in San Diego with her husband. Now that her children are grown, their two dogs keep her company while she sits at her computer writing stories. A native Californian, she enjoys the beach, loves to swim in the ocean, and for relaxation she daydreams and reads romances. Visit her at www.JillLimber.com!

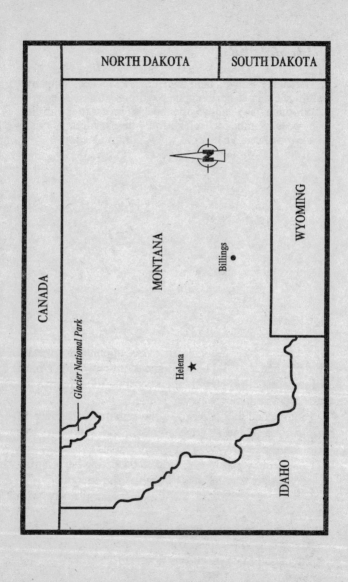

Chapter One

Today might qualify as the worst day of Jolie Carleton's life. If you didn't count last Saturday, when she'd been left standing at the altar in front of three hundred people.

Being jilted had left her more embarrassed than hurt. She'd had second thoughts about her intended for weeks. If she'd had the backbone to speak up it wouldn't have happened at all. It hadn't taken her long to recognize the incident as a major wake-up call.

Jolie sighed and stabbed at the remains of a piece of cheesecake. Saturday night she'd made a vow to live with courage, to do something outrageous every day and get a life, but so far fate seemed to be testing her. Getting a life was proving to be harder than she imagined.

Glumly she watched the sunset paint the sky with streaks of orange and purple behind Winslow's Garage across the street and tried to ignore the diner's other customers, who watched her with open curiosity.

The smell of fried onions hung in the warm air, and

the waitresses wore pink nylon uniforms with their name tags pinned over a fan of starched hankie. Ever since her car had been towed into Billings, Montana, Jolie had the strangest feeling she had entered a time warp.

She heard the door to the diner slap closed and looked up to see a blond version of the Marlboro Man talking to her waitress. Her breath caught in her chest as she fumbled her fork.

Over six feet tall, he had the wardrobe and the build of the icon plastered all over magazines. His broad shoulders filled out a worn sheepskin jacket, and his long legs were covered by blue jeans. He took off his cowboy hat and ran a broad hand through sun-bleached blond hair.

She exhaled a sigh of pleasure. He was eye candy at its finest.

He nodded at the cashier and smiled, displaying a set of even white teeth. Tanned skin crinkled at the corners of his deep-blue eyes, and a dimple dented one cheek. Drop-dead gorgeous, the man looked like a Hollywood version of the perfect cowboy.

The words *hunk* and *babe* drifted through her mind as she openly stared at the man, unable to look away.

He needed a shave. The stubble on his chin made him look even more masculine. She could imagine the rasp a beard like that would make against her skin.

Now she liked Montana even more than she had a moment ago. Feeling warm all over, she had to remind herself she'd sworn off men.

He glanced over and caught her gawking, open-mouthed. Jolie bent her head over her newspaper so her hair would hide her face.

Embarrassed to be caught gaping at a stranger, Jolie stared down at the want ads she had already read twice, then turned her head and dared a peek through a curtain of hair.

The cowboy walked past her with enough of a swagger to convince her he had just gotten off a horse, and took a seat at a booth in the rear of the diner.

Jolie dared one more glance in his direction, then turned her attention back to her problems. She needed a job, she told herself firmly, not a man who had the potential to star in a woman's fantasies.

She tried to ignore the man and think about her situation. Just outside of Billings, a deer had bounded across the highway. Swerving to avoid the animal, Jolie had skidded across the shoulder of the road and run into a telephone pole.

She could almost hear her father scolding her. *Jolie,* he would say, as if she were still sixteen years old, *never swerve to avoid an animal.*

Easy enough to say when you didn't have Bambi looking at you with those big startled eyes.

An hour ago, as she'd brushed the fine white dust that had exploded out of her car's air bag off her silk shirt, the mechanic at Winslow's had told her it might take three weeks to get the parts he needed for the repairs to her car.

His exact words had been, "Don't stock parts for these foreign jobs" in a tone implying she'd broken some kind of law in Montana by driving a car made in Germany.

Now what was she supposed to do? Her car was wrecked, her father had cancelled her credit cards, and her Aunt Rosie was off backpacking somewhere in New York state.

Jolie struggled to think positively and come up with a solution to her problem. Collision coverage would take care of the car, but the deductible she'd had to pay the mechanic to order parts and start work had left her with a measly fifteen dollars.

She refused to call her father in Seattle for help. He'd predicted this trip would be a disaster and forbidden her to go. She'd left anyway, disobeying him for the first time in her life.

Most children rebelled against their parents when they were in their midteens. Jolie had waited until she was almost twenty-five years old.

She should've stood up to her father a lot sooner. Because she always went along with whatever he wanted just to keep the peace, she'd almost ended up married to a man she didn't love.

How could she prove to herself she could be independent if she ran to her father for help at the first sign of trouble? Besides, she was still furious with him for cancelling her credit cards to try to keep her from leaving.

She *had* called New York and left a message for Aunt Rosie that she'd been delayed, but Rosie wasn't due back from her trip until Sunday.

Rosie's newest man must be the outdoorsy type. She tried to picture her chic aunt in a pair of boots and a backpack, but couldn't come up with the image.

Jolie propped the heels of her Ferragamo flats on her suitcase and traced the outline of the state on the plastic place mat. She had no option but to stay right here in Billings and wait for the car.

She needed a job.

Jolie had planned to look for employment when she returned from her visit with her aunt, but it looked like her first work experience would be right here.

Watching the waitress stop at the next table to pour coffee, Jolie figured she could manage to wait tables.

That would pay enough to cover her expenses until her car was ready. True, she had never served food, but she had planned parties and supervised caterers for her father often enough.

"More coffee, hon?" The waitress's name tag identified her as Helen.

"No, thanks. But I do need a job. Are there any openings here?"

Helen laughed, then her eyes narrowed and slid over Jolie's designer clothes, lingering on her gold jewelry. "Harry hasn't hired anybody in over fifteen years. The only reason I got the job is 'cause I'm his sister-in-law."

So much for the idea of waiting tables, Jolie thought.

Helen still hovered over her, staring. "What's your name?"

"Jolie Carleton."

Helen nodded. "Howdy, Jolie. Might be we could find something for you close by. You ever wait tables?"

"No." She'd never had a job.

Helen raised one thinly plucked eyebrow. "Been a short-order cook?"

"No." Jolie felt her spirits drop another notch.

"Any cashier experience?"

Only from the customer's side. "No."

"Well, honey, what have you done?"

By now Jolie figured Helen wouldn't be impressed with a list of her Junior League projects. "I have a degree in child development. Maybe I could work at a preschool."

Helen gave her a speculating look. "You ever actually take care of kids, Jolie?"

Finally she could say yes to something. "I've taken care of my cousin's children."

"How many?" she asked, her voice skeptical.

"Three."

"How old?"

Why would Helen care how old her cousin's children were? Jolie felt protective of the children, probably because her cousin was like a barn cat. She had her babies and after a month or two paid no attention to them, resuming her ski trips and visits to friends in Europe.

Reluctantly she said, "Five, three, and a baby." Jolie hoped this was leading somewhere.

Helen stared for another disconcerting moment, nodded as if she'd come to some kind of decision, then turned abruptly and walked away. Jolie watched her cross the café to the gorgeous cowboy.

Helen and the cowboy held a whispered conversation, glancing frequently back at Jolie. Now, what was *that* all about?

Knowing she was the subject of their conversation, Jolie didn't know where to look. She stared down at the newspaper want ads, folded up on the edge of the table.

The toes of two hand-tooled leather cowboy boots appeared in her line of vision. The faint scent of horse and hay curled up to her.

She looked up, pinned in place by the cowboy's incredible blue eyes. He was no longer smiling, and she could see lines of fatigue on his face. He looked older than she had first thought.

"Ms. Carleton?" His deep voice rolled over her like a fog across Puget Sound.

Startled, Jolie nodded and swallowed. "Yes?"

Griff took a minute to take in the whole package. What the heck was a beautiful woman dressed like her doing in Harry's Diner? he wondered.

"My name's Griff Price. I have a proposition for you."

He didn't miss the way her big brown eyes widened at his choice of words, and in spite of his foul mood he suppressed a smile.

"How do you do, Mr. Price?" Her speech was careful and polite, her expression wary.

Sleek and sophisticated, she reminded him of a Thoroughbred horse. Generations of carefully chosen bloodlines came together to produce a woman this magnificent. Good bone structure, sleek hair, clear eyes, fine skin and good muscle tone didn't happen by accident.

He was pretty good at sizing up women. He'd learned the hard way. She didn't look like a baby-sitter.

She looked like trouble.

But Griff was desperate. He had just acquired a nephew he hadn't even known existed, and his housekeeper, Margie, was leaving to take care of her sick sister for at least two weeks.

"Helen tells me you've had experience taking care of children." She nodded and continued to stare at him with those big chocolate-brown eyes.

It was hard to believe, looking at her. She had *city* and *society* written all over her, and he wanted no part of either. She had the look of his ex-wife. Expensive. Deirdre would never willingly take a job as a caregiver. She had been a taker, not a giver.

Women like Ms. Carleton didn't belong in Montana. This country was harsh, and it would chew you up and spit you out if you weren't as tough as old saddle leather.

Glancing nervously at Helen, who hovered two booths away, she cleared her throat and said, "Yes."

Griff barely remembered his question and realized he'd been staring at her. He also noticed Helen had hung around to listen, wiping up an already immaculate tabletop. Gossip was first on the menu at Harry's.

Griff turned his attention back to Ms. Carleton. "Helen also mentioned you're looking for work."

He rubbed at his temple, trying to dispel the headache that had blindsided him on the way to town.

Looking uneasy, she glanced at Helen again, then back to him. Finally she nodded, looking as jumpy as a cat in a roomful of rocking chairs.

He'd bet a week's wages she was running away from something. Women like her always left when things got tough. He knew that from experience. First his mother had run, then his wife.

But, he reminded himself grimly as he watched the way her small smooth hand toyed nervously with a gold chain necklace, he didn't have much choice. And Helen had said she had cared for her cousin's children. Unlike his wife, she must have a sense of family, and to Griff that meant something.

"I need a live-in baby-sitter for a few weeks." He watched her absorb that information.

Deirdre had run off two years ago with his brother. Until three weeks ago when Social Services had called about his nephew, Riley, he'd known nothing about the baby, or Deirdre and his brother's deaths.

She brightened a little. "Live in?"

"Yes, ma'am. I live a ways out of town." He knew her car had been wrecked and there was no way he could take the time to drive her back and forth to town every day.

"I see." She continued to twist up the gold necklace that hung down over her full breasts. Little lines of concentration furrowed her brow.

"I've got a ranch to run." He tapped the toe of his

boot against the linoleum, anxious to be on his way. He still had hours of work to do before his day would end.

Griff couldn't stay home with Riley. The ranch took up all his time, even when things were going smoothly. And things had not been smooth for quite a while.

Right now he had fence down in two spots. God knew how many head had wandered into the coulees. It could take days to find them all. His main stock tank had sprung a leak sometime in the past few days, and he had to get it fixed or spend hours hauling water. And just to round things out, the weatherman was predicting a hard, early winter.

Worst of all, he missed his dad with a fierce ache in the belly. He wanted the old man beside him, quietly reassuring him that everything would work out.

Griff yanked his wandering thoughts back to the problem at hand. He stared at Miss Carleton, squirming on the red vinyl seat. No one had answered his advertisement, and Margie was leaving this afternoon.

He was desperate, but he wasn't a fool. She was all wrong for the job, but he needed time to find a permanent baby-sitter. Margie had made it very clear from the day the baby arrived she was a housekeeper and hadn't hired on to raise kids. This woman could do the job for the short term, to buy himself some time.

"We need someone for a couple of weeks." He watched her as she considered his offer, and wondered if she would last even a week.

She nodded hesitantly. "Okay."

He felt a spurt of relief. He'd be damned if he'd explain more to her here. Everyone in the diner had an ear turned toward their conversation. Any conversation he had with her here would be all over town in minutes.

He'd been the topic of their gossip enough to last him the rest of his life.

If she had questions, they could talk in the truck. He didn't want Billings chewing on his personal business again.

On the way back to the ranch he would tell her only what she would need to know to do the job. She was a stranger who would be in and out of his life. She didn't need to know why Riley was living with him. His brother's betrayal and death cut deeply into his soul, and he didn't plan on sharing it.

Griff pushed his dark thoughts away. It wasn't something he liked to dwell on. Every time he saw his nephew he was reminded of the fact his wife had run off with his brother. She had refused to have Griff's child, but obviously hadn't felt that way about his brother.

Apparently, Jolie thought as she watched him press his fingers to his forehead, even though he'd offered her a job, she hadn't made a very good first impression.

She hadn't missed how he had emphasized the fact that the position came with a time limit. That was fine with her; all she needed was a temporary position.

Jolie was not going to react to the annoyed expression on Mr. Price's face as he stared at her. How often had she caved in to her overbearing father when he had scowled at her like that?

Courage, Jolie, she told herself.

Helen knew Griff Price, and she must think it was okay for Jolie to work for him or she wouldn't have suggested it. She cleared her throat and was about to suggest he sit down and have a cup of coffee.

"Well, are you coming?" The sole of his boot slapped impatiently against the worn flooring.

She did want the job, but found it easier to say she was going to live with courage, harder to actually do it. "Yes, let's—"

"Come on, it's late," he said gruffly, cutting her off.

He jammed his hat back on his head. Then in one fluid movement he picked up her jacket, tossed it to her, lifted her suitcase, turned and strode out of the diner.

Dumbfounded, she watched him disappear into the twilight with her bag.

He might be one of the best-looking men she had ever met, but he had the manners of a boor.

Hurriedly she slid out of her seat, pulled four dollars out of her precious hoard, then slapped the bills down on the table. Exasperated by his rude behavior, Jolie approached Helen, who was setting a nearby table.

"Excuse me, but do you know Mr. Price very well?"

Helen smiled and nodded. "Sure do. I went to high school with his daddy. He comes from a fine family. Prices been running the Circle P spread for almost a hundred years."

Jolie looked uncertainly at the door. "He didn't give me a chance to ask any questions," she said, more to herself than Helen.

Helen smiled. "Oh, don't worry—"

"You coming or not?" Everyone in the diner turned as Griff Price stuck his head in the door and hollered at her, cutting off what Helen was about to say. Then he left without waiting for her to answer.

Jolie felt the blood rise in her cheeks. She'd made him angry.

Helen gave Jolie a gentle push toward the door. "That boy's always in a hurry. Margie will fill you in when you get to his place. She's going to visit her sick sister, but you can talk to her before she leaves.''

So that was why he needed a baby-sitter, Jolie thought as she followed him out the door, her stomach tied in knots at the thought she'd annoyed him. His wife was leaving.

On her way out she hurriedly summed up what she knew about the man, still trying to decide if going with him was a reasonable plan.

He was married, from a good family and offering a job she knew she could do. She *had* decided to live with courage and do something outrageous every day. Now it seemed as though she was going to be put to the test.

Besides, Jolie thought, her other choice was to bed down in her car in Winslow's garage.

She assured herself if she didn't feel comfortable with the situation when she got to their home, she'd ask Margie Price to bring her back to the diner.

By the time Jolie got to the parking lot, he was at the passenger door hefting her bag into the back seat of the biggest pickup truck Jolie had ever seen. She stopped about five feet from the cowboy.

He pointed at the open door. ''Get in. I've got stock to tend to.''

Taken aback by his abrupt behavior, Jolie inched toward the truck. ''Don't you want references?'' she asked.

Not that she could give him any work references, but it seemed like a good question to ask before they got too far out of town.

He stared at her for a moment. ''No. Is there some good reason you're stalling?''

''No, I—''

''You told Helen you'd taken care of your family's

kids," he said cutting her off and frowning at her as if he thought she might have lied to him.

"Yes, I did," she said, not quite knowing how she should respond to his lack of courtesy. She shivered as the cold evening air penetrated her thin blouse.

"Good," he answered, with such a tone of relief in his voice she relaxed a little. "You do want the job, don't you?" he asked, still staring, his tone back to edgy.

Jolie paused for another moment to shrug into her jacket, then decided she was being foolish to hesitate. "Yes, I do."

Her other choices sucked.

"Okay." He took two strides to get to her, grabbed her around the waist, lifted her up and set her on the seat.

Breathless at the suddenness of his bold action and the feel of his hands on her, she scrambled to get her feet in before he closed the door on them.

She took a deep breath and watched him stride around to the driver's door, hop in, then turn the key in the ignition. The truck's engine started with a roar.

He muttered something under his breath and pulled out of the parking lot while she was still struggling to find her seat belt. Holding the shoulder strap, Jolie dug down behind the seat to locate the buckle.

Suddenly his big warm hand slid along her hip and fished the fastener out from behind the seat.

She felt a zing of sensation where he'd touched her, then immediately chided herself.

He was married.

And she had sworn off men.

She murmured a quick thank-you. Hoping he couldn't see her face flush, she managed to connect the two ends of the belt.

The silence in the cab grew until Jolie couldn't stand it anymore. "Is your home very far?"

He shifted on the seat and shrugged one shoulder. "Nope."

Jolie waited for more of an explanation, but apparently that was his whole answer. She'd have to try another subject. "Mr. Price, how many children do you have?"

He cleared his throat. "Griff."

Jolie turned to look at him. "I beg your pardon?"

"My name is Griff. There's one child."

Jolie nodded and waited for him to give her more information. He stared straight ahead at the road.

Her annoyance grew until after a few moments she decided one of them needed to show some manners, so she tried again. "Griff, is your child a boy or a girl?"

"Boy."

Jolie struggled to hold on to her temper. He acted like she was charging him by the word. "How old is your son?"

He started to answer when a ringing phone interrupted them.

He reached inside his jacket and pulled a cellular phone out of his shirt pocket.

Turning her head just a little, Jolie studied him in the gathering gloom. His expression darkened as he listened intently to whoever was on the other end of the line.

Scowling, he glanced at the clock set in the dashboard. "When?" he barked into the phone, tightening his grip on the instrument.

His intensity made her uncomfortable. The man certainly didn't believe in wasting time on conversation. Or manners. Jolie was accustomed to polite small talk, no matter how meaningless.

"Take care of that now." He barked into the phone.

Jolie shifted her gaze to stare out the window at the empty country and the sapphire sky as she listened to his one-word questions and answers. The landscape that had seemed beautiful and wild a few hours ago now appeared barren. She fought down the urge to ask him to take her back to the diner.

Don't be a fool, she thought. She was going to be courageous. Besides, she didn't have any options. She was starting to realize how easy her life had been when she'd let others make her decisions for her.

She chanted her new mantra to herself. Courage, I live with courage. And because of that courage, she had her first job. She had wanted to work right after college, but her father had always had a reason she should wait. A trip, a charity ball to organize, overseeing the redecoration of the house.

Griff turned off the main road. She glanced at him and decided she wouldn't let a little surliness get her down. She'd just have to work on those clever comebacks that always occurred to her an hour after she needed them.

She could see a house in the distance, sitting on a broad expanse of open plain. The huge building behind the house was probably a barn. Didn't ranches have barns?

She thought of a dozen questions, but when she glanced at Griff, who stabbed at the power button on his phone as if he was killing a venomous insect, she decided not to waste her breath.

She'd talk to Mrs. Price.

As he parked behind a small, battered, blue compact car, Jolie stared at the enchanting yellow-and-white Victorian house, complete with wraparound porch and gabled roof, and hid a smile.

The big sour cowboy who had driven her in from Billings did not belong in such an enchanting home. It looked too feminine and had too much charm. His wife must be a lovely woman.

Without a word he opened the driver's door and climbed out, then hauled her suitcase out of the back.

Jolie opened her door and slid out of the truck, following Griff up the front steps. She stepped through the open door and almost bumped into an old woman in the entry hall.

The woman jammed an ancient black pillbox hat with torn netting over her gray hair while she scolded Griff Price. "About time you got back. Now I got to drive in the dark."

She thrust a lethal-looking hat pin through the battered crown of her hat and glared up at him.

She glanced at Jolie. "Baby's asleep." Without saying another word, she headed out the door.

Baby? For some reason Jolie had pictured an older child. She watched the woman march down the steps and get in the blue car.

By this time Jolie was not the least bit surprised not to get an introduction.

Just as the old woman was closing her car door, Griff hollered down to her. "Hey, Margie, did that feed supplier call?"

Jolie spun around to stare at Griff Price. *That* was Margie?

Chapter Two

So much for making assumptions, Jolie thought. Obviously Margie was *not* Griff Price's wife.

Jolie tore her surprised look away from Griff and looked back to see Margie, driving like someone qualifying for the Indy 500, head out to the main road in a cloud of dust.

Not meeting her eye, Griff took off his hat and ran his hand through his hair. "She was in a hurry."

Jolie choked back a sarcastic remark. He turned to go back out the door, as if that was all the information Jolie needed.

Was he just going to leave her standing here? She stepped in front of him, grabbing the sleeve of his sheepskin jacket, blocking his path. "Wait a minute. Where are you going?"

He stared at her for a moment with those sky-blue eyes, then shook her hand off his arm and ran his hands tiredly over his face. "I told you. I have stock that needs tending."

Confused, Jolie looked around. "Is your wife here?"

His face hardened into a scowl. "No wife."

Jolie's hand dropped to her side, and she eyed the big cowboy. Now a few of the pieces of the puzzle that hadn't made sense fell into place.

She suspected she knew why he was acting so rude. His wife had left him with their child. He was hurting and he covered it up with anger. How many times had she watched her father do the same thing?

"I'm sorry." It sounded trite, but she couldn't think of anything else to say.

"Don't be." He said curtly and shrugged one shoulder as if he wanted her to think it didn't bother him. Abruptly he turned toward the stairs. "I'll show you the baby's room."

She followed him, her heels clicking on the bare wood of the stairs. He stopped at an open door and gestured for her to go ahead of him.

The only light in the room came from the hall. Jolie could see a crib in the corner and assumed Griff's son was asleep. Then, as her eyes became accustomed to the gloom, she saw movement in the small bed.

Jolie turned to ask Griff the child's name, and the words died on her lips.

He was gone.

He had left her standing alone in the doorway, with no information about his son. Jolie felt the outrage grow inside her.

How could he leave her standing here without even bothering to give her the baby's name? Angry or not, the man needed to pull himself together for the sake of his child.

Jolie flipped the light switch. The baby boy sat quietly in the corner of his crib, staring at her, his big blue eyes blinking against the sudden light. He had a head of blond curls and was going to grow up to look just like his daddy.

Jolie hoped he ended up with a better disposition.

"Well hello there, little guy," she said.

Staying where she was for a moment, she smiled at the child, afraid to approach too quickly and frighten him. She knew some babies were afraid of strangers.

He was about the size of her cousin's youngest child, so she guessed he must be about ten months old. "Did you just wake up?"

Jolie took her jacket off and laid it over the back of a chair. "My name is Jolie."

Slowly she moved into the middle of the room, then stopped about five feet from the battered crib. "I don't know your name because your daddy had to leave in a hurry." And he's a handsome, rude man, she added to herself.

The baby sat motionless, staring at her with his big blue eyes.

"So this is your room. I don't know where I'm supposed to sleep." The baby's room contained just the crib, an old wooden dresser and a single bed with a bare mattress.

No toys or stuffed animals littered the room. Griff's housekeeper must be a very tidy woman. "Where's all your stuff?"

The baby didn't move or change his facial expression at her inane conversation. He just continued to stare at her. She moved a little closer to the bed and watched him watching her.

"Are you ready to get up?" Jolie had no idea if he was waking from a nap, or had been put down for the night. She took another step toward the bed, feeling as though she was in the middle of a one-person, red-light-green-light game.

When he showed no signs of being alarmed by her presence, Jolie moved all the way to the bars of the crib. He was dressed in a blanket sleeper, and she could tell from where she stood that he needed a fresh diaper.

"How about we get you cleaned up and go find your daddy. I have some things I need to say to him," she said, not allowing her annoyance to show in her voice.

It wasn't the baby's fault that his father had no manners.

She lowered the side of the crib and reached in to get him. He allowed her to pick him up, and when she lifted him up against her chest, he put his head on her shoulder and wound his arms around her neck, then gave what sounded like a little sigh as he nestled into her body.

Jolie felt her heart turn over. In that instant she fell in love with a little boy whose name she didn't even know.

Jolie sat at the dining room table, her temper simmering just below the boiling point. Holding the quiet baby in her lap with one hand and, with the other, folding clean baby clothes she had discovered in the dryer, she waited for Griff Price to return.

Where was he? Didn't people who worked on a ranch quit when the sun went down? It had been dark for hours.

She slapped a tiny shirt down on the shiny tabletop. "There's no excuse for the way he walked out on me," she said to the baby, careful to use a cheerful conversational tone that masked her feelings.

"Leaving you with a stranger." Tossing the shirt into the basket, she yanked a faded sleeper out of the small pile.

She kissed the top of his head. "He didn't say ten words to me on the way here from the diner."

Jolie took a deep breath, trying to relax, then nuzzled the tumble of clean curls on the baby's crown. "How does he know I can be trusted with you?"

If he were her little boy she'd never leave him with someone she didn't know.

She'd given him his bath, fed him, and he was now ready to be put to bed. Together they had explored the house while she'd waited for her employer to return.

No matter how busy Griff claimed to be, the man should have been home early enough to spend some time with his son. She knew from her training nothing mattered more than the early bonding between a parent and child.

That was why she had spent so much time with her cousin's children when they traveled and left them in the care of their nanny for weeks at a time.

She assumed this little boy's mother had already deserted him. If she lived nearby, Jolie reasoned, the ex-wife would be caring for her son. Griff wouldn't have had to hire Jolie.

Jolie's thoughts shifted to the child she held. She was worried about the baby. He was too quiet.

He didn't try to crawl, and he didn't reach for things. He just watched her and clung to her when she picked him up. He didn't laugh or vocalize in any way.

Maybe it was because she was a stranger. Tomorrow, when he was used to her, he would probably be more active.

She glanced around the dining room. Something was not right about the home environment, either. Earlier, as she'd wandered through the house getting acquainted with the place, she'd felt uneasy.

The wonderful old Victorian was clean and extremely tidy, but there were no homey touches, no warmth. Nothing that hinted at the people who lived here. As if the clutter of everyday life, the things that told something about the residents, was not allowed to accumulate.

It bothered her. Not for Griff Price's sake. Whatever had made him such a closed-off grouch was his problem. Jolie's concern was all for the baby she held in her arms.

As she waited, she smoothed her hand over the little boy's fuzzy blanket sleeper and enjoyed the weight and warmth of him as he settled back against her lap. "I have some questions for your daddy."

He turned his head and looked up at her with his big blue eyes. "I don't even know your name." Jolie stroked the soft skin of his little cheek.

"I'm not even sure where your daddy wants me to sleep." She stroked his cheek again, and his eyelids blinked sleepily.

There was a bedroom next to the baby's room, but she didn't want to presume. After glancing into bedrooms, she couldn't even tell which room Griff slept in. Her suitcase still sat at the bottom of the stairs in the entryway.

Jolie turned the baby so he lay in the crook of her arm, and confided her anxiety at facing Griff Price with her questions. "Confrontation has never been my strong suit."

She chanted her new mantra for him. "I live with courage. Catchy, isn't it? For the next few weeks I'm going to take care of you, even if it means getting in your daddy's face."

Jolie discarded the idea Griff thought her so efficient she didn't need any guidelines. She suspected he had simply not bothered to tell her.

Did he expect her to do other work besides caring for the baby? There was no evidence of an evening meal. In fact, there was little food in the refrigerator. Before discovering baby clothes in the dryer, she wondered what the little guy would wear tomorrow.

The baby's head nodded against her arm, and she turned him and hoisted him up against her shoulder. He nuzzled into the curve of her neck, his little body relaxed as he slid into sleep. She stroked his back and fell a little more in love with him.

The longer Griff Price took to come home, the madder she got.

She continued to rub the baby's back. If she wasn't desperate for a job and a place to stay, she would demand he take her back to town the minute he walked in the door.

As soon as she had the thought she realized she was kidding herself. She couldn't leave until she straightened this man out about the way he was raising his son.

His cows seemed to mean more to him than his child. Griff Price's behavior was inexcusable.

The back door slammed, jerking her out of her thoughts. She looked up and spotted Griff coming through the door that led to the mudroom. He stopped at the kitchen sink, his broad back to her.

Jolie got up, holding the sleeping baby on her shoulder as she strode into the kitchen to give the man a piece of her mind.

He stood, his tall frame hunched over the sink, washing his hands. In the short time since she had met him she had forgotten what a big man he was.

He turned to look at her, surprise plain on his face. "Evening."

Had he forgotten she was in the house? She cleared

her throat and said in a low voice, "Actually, it's past evening."

He stared at her for a moment, then his glance slid briefly over his son, as if trying to place who they were. Finally he looked past her, over her shoulder.

What was he doing, checking the dark house to see if there was anyone else there he might have forgotten?

Jolie took a deep breath and reached for her courage, determined to pin him down. "Mr. Price, I have some questions I need answered now."

His expression became shuttered so quickly she blinked at the change in him.

He shifted his glance away from her face. "Okay. I'm listening." He picked a towel up off the counter to dry his hands.

Jolie put a protective hand up to cradle the sleeping child's head, as if contact with the baby could keep her focused on what she planned to say to him. "You left without telling me the baby's name or anything about him."

"His name is Riley." Griff seemed to be searching his mind for something else to say. "He's ten months old."

She watched him focus on something behind her again, and his shoulders slumped in a defeated movement as he leaned his hips against the cabinet. "You're leaving."

Jolie glanced over her shoulder and saw that he stared at her suitcase. "Oh, no. I'm staying. My suitcase is there because you didn't bother to tell me which room is mine."

She couldn't leave.

Not just because she didn't have any money.

Griff Price needed her, whether he realized it or not.

And for a lot more than changing his son's diapers. His expression told her how badly he *thought* he needed her, and he didn't know the half of it.

No one had ever needed Jolie before, not like this.

She would stay, not for him, but for the precious little boy asleep in her arms. She hadn't missed the fact he hadn't taken even a moment to ask after his child.

"We need to talk." She suspected before long he would regret he hadn't taken her back to town tonight.

Griff let out a sigh as he watched the stubborn set of Jolie Carleton's sweet little chin. Still fighting his headache, he thought sourly, was there a phrase he hated more than *we need to talk?*

He eyed the beautiful, frazzled-looking woman standing there holding his nephew. In the few hours since he had met her he had tried to forget what a fine-looking woman she was.

Griff eyed the set of her jaw and knew before the words were out of his mouth he would regret asking. "About what?"

Her lovely mouth dropped open as if he had asked an astounding question. She caught herself gaping at him and closed her jaw with a snap of perfect white teeth.

Taking a deep breath, she glanced down at Riley, then hissed at Griff. "About your responsibilities, Mr. Price."

Well, he had a million of those, that was for sure. "What responsibilities would those be?"

Her pale fine skin flushed. "This baby!"

She was no longer trying to keep her voice down. Riley jerked awake, his head coming off her shoulder.

Griff didn't want to talk about his nephew. Not tonight. If she had just kept her voice down, Riley would still be asleep.

He skewered her with a look designed to intimidate. "Wrong, Ms. Carleton. I hired you to take care of Riley. He's *your* responsibility."

Griff turned away from the dumbfounded look on her face, crossed through the house to the stairs and picked up her bag.

He didn't want to explain anything. Talking about the baby would lead to talking about his wife and his brother. That was a subject he didn't plan to cover, especially with a stranger.

He needed some aspirin and a good night's sleep. Tomorrow would be another too-full day. He'd still be out on the range tonight if the moon hadn't set.

As he got to the top of the stairs he heard her determined footsteps just behind him. He glanced over his shoulder and held back another sigh as he watched her march up the stairs.

She looked like a woman with a mission. It didn't take a genius to figure out she hadn't liked his answer.

That scowl he had used on her downstairs worked on his hired hands but didn't seem to phase Jolie Carleton.

Save me from crusading females, Griff thought as he put her suitcase just inside the door of the bedroom next to the baby's room. He straightened up and braced himself for another round.

She sailed past him without a word, stepped into Riley's room and closed the door firmly behind her.

Surprised to find, in spite of his headache, he was a little disappointed she hadn't faced him down again, he stood and stared at the closed door.

He had no intention of telling her about Deirdre or Jake, but he had enjoyed the flush on her cheeks and the flash of anger that ruffled her composed exterior.

In the diner she had come across as cool and collected.

With all that temper simmering below the surface, she might prove to be more passionate than he had first supposed.

Standing out in the hall, he heard her walking back and forth across the bare wood floor, murmuring to Riley.

Griff continued to stare at the closed door as he wondered what it would be like to peel the fragile silk of her blouse off and see all that fine pale skin turn rosy with arousal. His body reacted to the thought, and he smiled.

This just might turn out to be an interesting couple of weeks.

He could hear her through the door, still muttering to the baby. Griff rubbed his hand over the tired muscles of his neck. He was pretty sure the discussion regarding his responsibilities wasn't over.

When a woman said she wanted to talk to a man, it meant she talked until she got the man to agree.

Tired as he was, he found himself looking forward to tomorrow night.

Chapter Three

After spending less than twenty-four hours with Riley, Jolie was concerned about the little guy. Maybe he was coming down with something, but he was too quiet.

She needed to talk to Griff tonight. It was already well past dark and Griff Price had not returned to the house. He had left before she'd awakened this morning. Now Riley was almost ready for bed, so that meant a whole day with no contact between father and son.

She suspected Griff was staying away so he wouldn't have to talk to her.

It was her fault. She should have stayed calm last night instead of closing the door in his face, but she had been so angry she would have said things he wasn't ready to hear.

He thought the baby was her responsibility. His announcement had told her a lot. Could he actually think he didn't need to have contact with his son at this point in the child's life? That a temporary baby-sitter could take the place of both parents?

Into a bowl she put fresh greens from the garden outside the mudroom and glanced down at Riley, who sat quietly on an old towel in the middle of the kitchen floor.

Although Riley watched her all the time, he didn't make sounds or smile. Jolie knew his eyesight and hearing were okay, she had given him some basic tests and he had responded by following her movements and turning to sounds.

She put the greens aside and took two wooden spoons out of a crock by the stove, placing them on the towel beside the baby.

"Pick them up, Riley. They're for you. It's okay to touch them." She smiled at him, encouraging him with a nod of her head.

Riley looked at the spoons, then back up at her. He didn't reach for the utensils, just continued to watch her.

She waited for a few moments, and when he didn't move, she found a set of metal measuring spoons in a drawer, gave them a shake so they all clanked together, then laid them beside the other spoons.

"Don't they make a fun noise?" she cooed, and bent over him, giving them another shake. "Take them."

As she dangled the spoons, his gaze lingered for a moment longer on them, then returned to her face. This time she noticed his fingers opened and closed, but he still didn't reach out.

She laid them down on the towel beside him. "When you're ready, you pick them up."

As Jolie returned to dinner preparation, the suspicion that something might be wrong emotionally with Riley tore at her heart.

She had no idea how to tell Griff that she suspected a problem. Her greatest apprehension was that Griff might not care. Could he be that detached from his own child? Or did he already suspect that something might be wrong, and he couldn't accept a less than perfect child?

She wasn't trained for this. She needed to take Riley to a pediatrician and get a professional opinion. Babies his age, normal babies, had only two speeds. Full tilt or sound asleep. They explored everything with insatiable curiosity.

Jolie's hands stilled and she realized she had slipped back into her old way of thinking. There were things she could do, if she had the courage.

For instance, there were no toys in the house, no bright mobiles or wall hangings in his room to catch Riley's interest.

When she stayed with her cousin's children, sometimes it took an hour for her and the nanny to pick up their toys and games, even when the maid pitched in.

Perhaps Riley's problem was a lack of stimulation in his environment. Most children formed an attachment to a special blanket or stuffed toy they had dragged around everywhere they went. He couldn't do that because he didn't have anything.

The only time she got any reaction from Riley was when she picked him up. Then he clung to her like a limpet on a rock at the shoreline. The feel of his little hands grabbing her almost broke her heart.

The back door slammed and Griff came into the kitchen through the mudroom.

Riley watched Griff come in, but showed no reaction.

At the other extreme, her pulse leaped at the sight of him. Annoyed at the purely physical reaction the man evoked in her, she smacked the metal bowl down on the counter harder than she had intended.

He glanced at her, an eyebrow raised in question.

Then his eyes slid slowly over her apron, eyeing her as if she were wearing a lacy item from Victoria's Secret instead of the ancient faded smock she'd found in a drawer.

Every nerve ending in her body seemed to tingle.

Flustered by his perusal and her reaction, she met his gaze. Courage, she thought, have courage.

She wasn't going to let him intimidate her.

Her ex-fiancé used to do that to get her off a subject he didn't care to pursue. But Charles had never been able to derail her with just a look.

Jolie shivered. Those blue eyes of his made her stomach do little flip-flops.

"Evening." He held her eye for another disarming moment, then glanced down briefly at Riley before turning to the sink. He didn't speak to his son.

"Good evening." She kept her tone light and tried to keep her mind on the discussion she intended to have with him during dinner.

He had on a denim shirt that pulled across his shoulders as he reached to turn on the water. The color made his blue eyes even bluer. Deeply tanned skin made his hair looked gilded in the bright kitchen light.

In spite of how good he looked, Jolie didn't miss the fact that lines of fatigue, so apparent yesterday, had deepened around his eyes and mouth.

Jolie watched the baby as Griff finished washing up. Riley displayed only a simple curiosity at the new person who had entered his presence. No smiles or squeals of happiness at seeing a familiar face, no anticipation of attention.

Griff had shown no interest in the child beyond a cursory glance.

They acted as if they were strangers.

Jolie felt a moment of panic. She wasn't qualified to deal with this situation. How could she get Griff and Riley together?

Courage, she told herself sternly, you live with courage. You may not have the training for this, but you're all they have to save them.

When she had vowed to have courage and do something outrageous every day, she had never considered taking on something as complicated as repairing the damaged relationship between a man and his son.

She had thought more along the lines of working up the nerve to get a tattoo in a place no one else would see.

The daunting task of fixing this parent-child relationship made the thought of decorating her hip with a small tattoo seem too trivial to think about.

But, she reminded herself, she was all this man and his son had. Jolie didn't see Griff as the kind of person who would go looking for help.

She was pretty sure he didn't know he *needed* help.

She was absolutely sure he wouldn't *want* her help.

But, she told herself, you've dealt with your own father all these years. They didn't come much more difficult than Richard Carleton.

The key here was for Griff to think that becoming more involved with Riley was really his idea. Jolie could be very underhanded if it meant a better life for the baby.

She plastered a smile on her mouth, turned and faced Griff as he rinsed the soap off his hands. "Dinner is almost ready."

She didn't miss his suspicious look.

Jolie lifted two plates out of the cupboard and set them on the counter.

He watched her for a moment, then said, "I have to make two calls, then I'm going back out."

Concentrating his gaze on the towel, he acted as if the task of drying his hands required his full attention.

She wasn't going to let him get away, not now, while she was having a hard time holding on to her resolve.

Forcing herself to adopt a reasonable tone, she phrased her response as a question. "You can take time to eat, can't you?"

He stared at her while he seemed to consider his answer. "Will it be ready in ten minutes?" he asked in a wary voice.

"Yes." She'd make sure of it. He was trying to put distance between them and she needed to get started on him.

She only had two weeks.

"Ring the bell." He gestured to a round metal contraption with a pull chain set high on the kitchen wall.

Then he stepped around Riley as if the baby were a piece of furniture, and left the kitchen without sparing a word for his son.

Jolie stood staring at the empty door frame, unable to believe what had just happened. He hadn't even taken a moment to pat his son on the head.

Griff Price had to be the most aggravating person she had ever encountered. It was as if he refused to have any more human contact than was absolutely necessary.

She suspected if she suggested they work out a series of signals with the bell so that they wouldn't have to talk to each other he'd like the idea.

How could Riley thrive in this atmosphere? She scooped the baby off the floor and gave him a fierce hug as he nestled into her arms.

"Don't worry," she said into his curls, "I'm not leaving until he realizes how precious you are. And what you need," she added, hoping keeping the promise wouldn't take more courage than she possessed.

Jolie rocked him in her arms for a few more moments and crooned silly endearments, then put him back down.

If she didn't have dinner ready, Griff would leave and she would miss a chance to talk to him. Hurrying through the preparation, she finished up and tugged on the bell chain.

The loud clang made her jump.

What an annoying noise, she thought as she pulled out her chair and sat.

Griff slid into his chair and forked a bite off the plate of fresh greens topped by a broiled, sliced chicken breast. After a few bites he said, "This is good. What's for dinner?"

She thought he must be kidding, but so far she hadn't seen him display a glimpse of a sense of humor. "*This* is dinner."

"Is there any more?" He looked at her with a hopeful expression.

Jolie shook her head. "No. Sorry."

What was wrong with her? She should have realized a man who worked outside all day would need more than a salad for dinner. She pushed a basket of bread toward him.

At least he was talking. If they had to start with food, that was fine with her. "What kind of food do you like for dinner?"

He thought for a minute. "Steak. The chest freezer in the mudroom is full."

Of course he would like beef. He grew them, didn't he? She hadn't looked in the chest freezer that took up half of one wall.

The top of the appliance was piled with newspapers and bags of empty beer cans. Her hands had been full with Riley and she hadn't taken the time to clear it off so she could check inside. She had discovered the ice-incrusted package of chicken breasts in the freezer section of the refrigerator in the kitchen.

"We need to talk about Riley." Jolie laid her fork on her plate.

He glanced down at the baby, who stared back at him. "What about him?"

Jolie started with something small and worked her way up. "He doesn't have any toys."

Griff shrugged. "Isn't he too young for toys?"

"Not at all. He needs things to help develop his hand-eye coordination."

He frowned and threw her a skeptical look, then shrugged.

Jolie groped around for something else to say to keep him talking to her. "And he has very few clothes."

His features tightened up. "Can you drive a stick shift?"

"Yes." She noted the change in his expression and wondered if money was a problem for him.

She'd gladly charge everything the baby needed, but the only thing her credit cards were good for now was scraping gum off the bottom of her shoe.

He waved his hand. "Take the truck and get what he needs."

Embarrassed to ask, she saw no alternative. "I'll need money."

He rolled on his hip and worked his wallet out of a back pocket, pulled out a handful of bills and put the money in the middle of the table.

"What about a baby's car seat? Do you have one of

those?'' There hadn't been one in the truck he had driven last night.

Jolie watched Griff's features tighten up even more as he shook his head.

Getting answers out of him was a painful process. What did he do, lay the baby on the seat of that big truck of his? She felt a spurt of anger at his disregard for his son's safety.

He pushed his chair back, and she grabbed his arm to stay him, feeling the hard, warm muscle under the fabric of his shirt. ''There's more I need to say before you leave again.''

She had waited all day to talk to him, and she didn't have time to put this off.

He looked down at her hand clutching his arm and she felt the hard muscle under her fingers tense. ''Hurry up and get it over with. I've got work to do.''

Jolie dropped her hand, sorry that she had touched him like that. He obviously didn't like it.

''I'm worried about Riley.''

Griff looked quickly at the baby, then back at Jolie. ''He looks fine to me. Is he sick?''

Jolie took a deep breath. No parent wanted to hear that something might be wrong with their child. She chose her words carefully.

''No. Physically he appears to be fine. But you must have noticed that he doesn't crawl or reach for things.''

Griff sat very still, studying fingers splayed on his knees. What was he looking for, bamboo strips under his fingernails? she thought sourly. He acted as if he was being tortured.

Finally he glanced up at her and spoke. ''Isn't he too young to do those things?''

"No. He should be reaching and crawling and even pulling himself up to stand."

Griff rubbed his palms against his blue-jean-clad thighs and stared at Riley.

Jolie waited for him to absorb the information, then asked gently, "What has his pediatrician told you about his development?"

"Pediatrician?" He looked at her blankly.

"Do you take him to your regular doctor?" Maybe he used a family practice doctor.

Griff shrugged, still staring at the baby. "I haven't taken him to the doctor."

Jolie was appalled. What about his well-baby checks and vaccinations? "Never?"

"I just got him, okay?"

Jolie's head jerked up at his rough tone that didn't quite mask the pain underneath. "What?"

Just got him? It hadn't occurred to her that Riley might have been living elsewhere. She assumed his ex-wife had left him and the child.

"You heard me." He clamped his mouth shut so tightly a muscle twitched in his jaw.

She had heard him, and what he said made a big difference. She decided to try another approach. "Look, I know you think I'm prying, but there are things I need to know if I'm going to take care of Riley."

Agitated, Griff told himself he had wasted too much time eating the rabbit food she passed off as dinner, and he had heard more than enough talk. She may have a degree in some field about children, but she didn't know what she was talking about.

Dread he didn't want to face had him standing up so fast his chair tipped over and crashed against the floor.

Furious at himself for reacting to her, he jerked the

chair upright and turned on her. "You *are* prying. There's nothing wrong with the kid. I hired you to feed him and watch him. That's all."

If he didn't get out of the kitchen he was going to say something he'd regret about her nosy ways. He walked out the door, leaving her with her pretty little mouth hanging open.

Griff stopped in the middle of the yard and ran his hands through his hair. It was a wonder he could keep his temper at all around her. She was a managing kind of female with a body that made him want to weep.

There was nothing wrong with Riley. If there had been, the social worker would have said something.

The problem was her. It had to be her. He couldn't handle it if it wasn't.

Exhaustion dragged at him. It would be hours tonight before they finished riding the fence line. He tipped his head back and stared at the stars, just starting to show in the evening sky.

He had awakened several times last night with the thought that she was sleeping just down the hall. Usually when he was working as hard as he had been lately, he slept like a rock.

He was horny, tired and hungry. None of the conditions improved his disposition.

Last night, on his way back to the house, he had decided that he wasn't going to sleep with her. He had learned the hard way that the hotter his blood ran for a woman, the colder his bed was when she left.

The decision seemed reasonable until he was in the same room with her.

To get his mind off her sweet little body, he thought about what she had said about his nephew.

She was wrong about Riley. The kid was fine. Just quiet, like him.

There was such a thing as too much education, and he suspected *that* was Jolie Carleton's problem. She wanted to see things that weren't there.

Riley had looked okay to Griff, sitting in the middle of the kitchen floor. The kid didn't need toys. He didn't play with the spoons and stuff he had. And if he hadn't started to crawl yet, that just made her job easier. She didn't have to chase after him.

Better she should spend her time cooking a decent meal, he thought sourly, hopeful the boys hadn't eaten the whole pot of chili he had smelled when they had come in.

Did she think he could ride all day and get filled up eating sissy food for dinner?

If Griff had any sense at all he'd have one of his hands drive her back to town tonight.

But he couldn't spare anyone, he told himself, and until he found a baby-sitter he couldn't spare her.

He rolled his stiff shoulders. It had taken all day to find all the cows that had wandered into the coulees, and he still had a lot of work to do. The moon was so bright they could mend the last of the fence tonight.

Griff headed for the bunkhouse to round up the evening crew.

Tomorrow he'd find time to place another ad in the paper for a baby-sitter. Someone like Margie.

Old.

Cantankerous.

And blessedly quiet.

The sooner he got rid of Miss Jolie Carleton, the better off he was going to be.

* * *

Jolie stood in the dark mudroom and watched Griff as he stalked across the yard. The newly risen moon gave off enough of a glow that she saw him stop and tilt his head back to stare up into the sky.

Moonlight turned his hair to silver. She wouldn't have been surprised if he started howling like a wolf.

He might think of himself as a loner, not wanting anyone intruding into his life, but she hadn't missed the look of fear and pain that had crossed his features when she had mentioned she was worried about Riley.

She suspected this man was carrying around some deep wounds he didn't want anyone to see.

Even if he didn't want to show it, he had feelings for his baby. Now she had to figure out a way to get the two of them together. It didn't take a genius to see how closed off and stubborn the man was. Whatever she decided to do, he would need to think it was his idea in the first place.

When Griff disappeared around the side of the barn, Jolie turned back to the kitchen. Riley was on the floor, just where she had left him.

She went toward him to scoop him up. He didn't make a sound, but his little chin quivered.

Jolie felt a rush of emotion as she hugged his little body and felt him settle against her shoulder. "Did you think I wasn't coming back?"

She nuzzled his neck. "I'm going to make sure your daddy will be able to hug you and love you just as much as you need him to before I leave."

She shifted the baby so that she could see his face. "Because he needs you just as much as you need him."

Planting a kiss on the end of his little nose, she pulled him back into a fierce hug. "He just doesn't know it yet. I'm staying until he figures it out."

Chapter Four

Griff walked into the kitchen and waited until Jolie turned to look at him. She was a fine-looking woman, he thought. He held out the keys to his truck.

Just as Jolie reached for them with her slim, smooth hand, he pulled them back. "Are you sure you know how to drive a stick shift?"

His move obviously annoyed her, and her eyes flashed at his challenge. "Yes. I had a boyfriend in college who had a manual transmission."

"What kind of car?" Not all transmissions were the same.

She shrugged. "I don't know. A sports car."

"I think you need a lesson."

She started to say something, then just stared at him.

Why didn't he just let her go? She could get the hang of the truck before she got to the main road.

He chided himself for even asking the question. You're not letting her go because you want to sit beside her up in the cab of your truck and spend some time inhaling that incredible perfume she dabbed on this morning under her sexy sweater.

She stared him down, her chin jutting forward. "All right. If you're worried about your truck, I'll take a lesson."

He resisted the urge to tip that little chin up and find out how she tasted.

"I'll get the truck. Meet me out front in five minutes."

Griff trotted down to the tractor barn and drove his truck to the front of the house.

Jolie came out carrying the baby. "Here."

She thrust the baby into his arms, then opened the back door to the cab and climbed in. Griff held Riley awkwardly with both hands. He ignored the baby to concentrate on Jolie. He enjoyed the view as her trousers pulled taut across her very fine butt.

She turned and held out her hands. "Give him to me, and I'll strap him in."

She put him in the middle of the back seat and tightened the seat belt around him.

"That will have to do until we buy a car seat." She scooted over to the door and turned to climb down, giving Griff an encore.

He cleared his throat. "Okay. Go ahead and get in the driver's seat."

Jolie went around and hoisted herself back into the truck while Griff hopped in on the passenger side. When she strapped on her seat belt he noticed that her feet wouldn't reach the pedals.

"Hold on." He grasped the buckle of her seat belt, his hand brushing her hip, and snapped the clasp open.

She jumped and glared at him. "What are you doing?"

"If you're going to drive, your feet need to reach the floor." He leaned over, his head practically in her lap, and grabbed the bar at the base of her seat, scooting the bench seat forward.

Damn, the woman smelled good. "Try it now."

She had one foot on the brake and one on the clutch. When he glanced up, her cheeks were pink. Ah. The lady wasn't as cool as she let on. Griff smothered a smile.

He showed her the gear pattern, then took her through it a few times.

"Okay, start her up."

With the tip of her pretty pink tongue between her teeth, she turned the key and shifted into First. She let out the clutch too fast and the truck leaped forward, sputtered and stalled.

Jolie turned to check on the baby. "It makes me nervous that he isn't in a car seat."

Her sweater pulled taut against her breasts as she twisted in her seat. It felt like the temperature in the cab had gone up twenty degrees.

Griff adjusted his hat and cleared his throat. "Well, as soon as you get the hang of this you can take care of that."

Jolie said, "Right," through gritted teeth. She started the engine, let out the clutch and smoothly pulled away from the house, then turned her head toward him and smiled.

Damn she was pretty when she smiled.

"Just head out to the main road." He gave her a few more pointers on when to shift.

She was doing okay. If he didn't get out of the truck soon his attraction to her was going to be obvious to everyone.

"Now stop and turn around." Need made his tone harsh.

"Is anything wrong?" She glanced over at him.

"No. Drop me off in front of the barn." As soon as the truck came to a stop he bailed out and didn't look back.

Jolie watched him stalk away and then turned to Riley. "Your daddy sure is hard to figure out."

She shook off the feeling that she had done something to annoy him and concentrated on her driving.

She'd counted the money Griff had given her last night, made a list of stores from the phone book and planned her shopping trip. Now she was in an arena where she excelled. Shopping was something she understood. She'd never done it with a limited budget, but she was ready for the challenge.

She searched the street names and finally located the one she was looking for, pulling to a stop in front of a resale shop for children.

She undid Riley's seat belt, then hurried into the store through the cold morning air. After entering and closing the door behind her, she hesitated, resting her chin on the top of Riley's head.

A bored-looking teenage girl with a metal stud in her lip was behind the counter staring out the front plate-glass window.

"Good morning." Jolie tried not to stare at the metal adorning the girl's face.

The teenager shrugged.

Well, Jolie thought, no help would be coming from that direction. She turned her attention to her mission.

The store smelled musty. She'd never been in a resale shop before. Maybe they all smelled this way, she thought as she surveyed the jumble of clothes, toys and equipment.

She could do this. After all, her new motto was to live with courage, wasn't it?

As she wandered past the racks, she spotted a corner, set aside for children to play, that looked reasonably clean. She sat the baby down on the colorful squares of carpet, pulled a few toys within his reach, which he ignored, his eyes never leaving her.

She gave him a smile, leaned down and kissed his soft hair and said, "I'll be right back."

There were car seats and strollers in one corner. The best deal was a seat that looked sound but grubby. She shuddered a little and reminded herself of the amount of money she had to spend. She could do this. After all, it just needed a good scrubbing. No problem.

Gingerly Jolie picked up the car seat and carried it to the front of the store. "I'll just leave this here while I pick out some other things."

The girl glanced over at her and shrugged one shoulder. "Whatever," she said in a thoroughly bored tone.

Jolie suppressed a smile. Only a teenager could pull off that kind of apathy.

She walked back to where the baby sat. His eyes followed her. "Are you doing okay, buddy? I'm right here."

He showed no sign of emotion as she walked past him over to a rack of clothes marked twelve to eighteen months. As she decided on each item of clothing, she brought it over and held it up to him.

One little shirt, the exact color of his eyes, reminded her of another pair of blue eyes that had looked her over last night and this morning, raising her blood pressure by several notches.

She had ignored Griff's looks and would continue to do so. Her project was Riley.

The last thing she needed so soon after her disastrous wedding day was another romance. Even if she was living in the same house with the best-looking man she had ever met.

Resolutely she returned to the selection of baby clothes. Denim overalls and pants, long-sleeved knit shirts. Mostly red and blue, so the outfits could mix and match. With so little to spend, things needed to be interchangeable.

She found a brand-new soft-blue blanket with satin binding, sleepers, and a knit cap and mittens, adding them to her pile.

After spending some time selecting a jacket, she peeked around the rack to check on the baby. He was watching for her, and she thought she noticed a look of relief when he caught sight of her.

She smiled at him, drew back behind the rack for a moment, then stuck her head out again and said "Boo!"

She couldn't be sure, but it looked as if he was going to smile.

Watching him closely, she repeated the action several more times until his lips curved up in a tentative smile.

Exhilarated by this first small show of emotion, Jolie walked over and picked him up, hugging him to her chest, then pulling back to kiss his cheek.

She nuzzled his neck and murmured in a thick voice, "There's a happy little boy in there, sweetheart. We just have to find him."

Not wanting to break the special moment, she held him as she searched through several baskets. Jolie picked out a few toys, then carried her purchases to the counter.

The young sales clerk totaled the sale, acting as if she

was doing Jolie an enormous favor. Perching Riley on her hip, Jolie dragged the seat out to the truck and had to come back for the clothes. Miss Personality went back to staring out the window, never bothering to ask if she might help carry things to the truck.

Jolie wondered if she had been so self-centered at that age, and decided she probably had.

She put the bag of clothes on the floor and sat the baby on the driver's seat, then went around to the passenger side and tried to angle the car seat into the back.

"Whoa, little lady, let me help you with that."

Jolie swung around and found a teenage cowboy, complete with boots and a Stetson hat smiling at her.

"Looks like you need a hand."

She stepped back, and he wrestled the seat into the truck. She had needed a hand. "Thanks."

He glanced over at Riley as he pulled out the seat belt to secure the base. "This rig is from the Price place, isn't it."

"Yes, it is."

"So, that's Wild Man's kid."

Wild Man? Griff's nickname was Wild Man? It didn't fit, at least not the Griff Price Jolie had met. She stared at the cowboy as he strapped the base of the seat firmly in place.

His voice broke into her thoughts. "There you go." He backed out and tipped his hat to her.

"Thank you Mr...."

"Eric, Miss..." He flashed her a grin.

They both turned at the sound of rapping on glass. The sales clerk from the store was glaring at them from the front window.

Eric stopped flirting with a speed that told Jolie who his girlfriend was. "Whoops. Gotta go."

"Thank you, Eric." She hid a smile as he sauntered into the store.

She covered the car seat with the blanket, then picked Riley up and strapped him into the seat, tightening the harness until he was securely strapped in.

"There you go, buddy. So, they call your daddy Wild Man. How did he ever get a nickname like that?"

Riley blinked at her, yawned and settled back against the seat.

Jolie drove to the diner to ask Helen about a pediatrician. She fought the big truck into a reasonable facsimile of a parallel park just as Helen came up the sidewalk. Jolie stood by the open door and waved to the waitress.

Helen approached the truck and peeked curiously into the back seat at the sleeping baby. "My goodness, he looks just like his daddy did at that age."

"Wild Man?" Jolie said in a dry voice.

Helen nodded. "He had that nickname for as long as I can remember. It fit."

Jolie still didn't see the name fitting Griff, but she didn't say anything, not wanting to get sidetracked from her original purpose.

"Helen, I want to thank you for recommending me for the job."

She shot Jolie a speculative look. "You're welcome, honey. I think it'll work out good for both of you."

She didn't know if Helen meant the situation would be good for Jolie and Riley, or Jolie and Griff, but either way she wasn't going into that right now. Jolie sensed the very real possibility that if she said anything she would be the topic of gossip. The feeling left her uncomfortable.

Helen smoothed the front of her pink uniform. "I'm

starting my shift. Come on in and I'll fix you a sandwich." She gestured toward the diner.

"No, thanks. I need to find a pediatrician for the baby. I stopped by to see if you could give me a name."

"He's sick?" Helen asked in a worried voice, glancing at Riley.

"No, it's for a well-baby check."

Helen looked at her as if she'd lost her mind. "Why in the world would you pay a doctor to check a baby when you know he isn't sick?"

Jolie didn't have time to debate the issue so she ignored the question. "Is there a pediatrician you could recommend?"

"Sure. There are a couple of them in the medical building over by the hospital. I heard the one with the foreign name was pretty good."

Jolie smiled, thanked Helen and climbed back in the truck. The one with the foreign name. She'd look up doctors in the yellow pages and try to figure that out when she got home.

Riley never woke up on the trip back to the ranch. At first Jolie checked on him in the rearview mirror every minute or so, then settled in to the drive and took only an occasional glance at the baby. He slumped against the side of the car seat, his curly blond head resting against the head support.

He really was a beautiful child, but then, how could he miss? His daddy was the best-looking man Jolie had ever laid eyes on. She sighed. Too bad he didn't have a personality to match his looks.

As she bumped down the rutted turnoff to the ranch, she noticed things she had missed before in the dark. The outbuildings all looked newer than the house. There were corrals beyond the barn, and on the opposite side of the house was a single-story, long building with lots of windows. A cowboy sauntered out, and Jolie decided that must be the bunkhouse.

She pulled up in back of the house and opened the back door of the huge cab, then climbed on the running board and wrestled the sleeping baby out of the cab.

"Need a hand, ma'am?"

She glanced behind her and saw the man she had spotted coming out of the bunkhouse. Were all cowboys so polite? She remembered Griff's gruff, rude behavior last night. Well, most cowboys.

"Thanks. I can manage the baby if you would get the bags and bring them in."

He tipped his hat and smiled. "Sure thing."

She glanced behind her, a little unsure of the best way to step back off the running board and keep her balance with her arms full. A strong pair of hands on her waist guided her down off the running board, and she didn't miss the spark of appreciation in the young man's eyes when she turned to thank him.

The cowboy's reaction made her feel good. Being left at the altar had done nothing for her self-esteem. She smiled at him, and he hurried ahead of her to open the door.

"Thanks, ah…" she whispered over the sleeping Riley's head, not knowing the man's name.

"Chris, ma'am."

She winced at his address. They were probably the same age. "Jolie, please."

Again the grin. "Jolie."

She turned and carried Riley up to his crib, then hurried downstairs. Chris had deposited all her purchases on the kitchen table.

"Anything else? How about I put the truck away for you?"

"That would be great, but I need the baby seat out first."

"No problem. You want it in here?"

"No, just put it on the back porch."

Chris tipped his hat. "No problem. You need anything else, you just call over to the bunkhouse. I'm working nights this week."

She assumed the cows slept at night and so did the cowboys. Jolie went to work washing clothes and toys, then fixed herself a sandwich.

She wondered what Griff did for lunch.

She hadn't thought to ask. There wasn't anyplace for miles to grab lunch. Reminded of his appetite, she cleared off the top of the freezer, bagging up the newspapers and beer bottles and cans, then poked among the white packages until she found one labeled steak. She wasn't going to give Griff a chance to complain about the lack of food a second time.

In fact, she thought, perhaps food was a way to a truce with her surly boss. They certainly hadn't gotten off to a good start, but it might be a way to get them back on track. She definitely needed to try a different approach.

Confrontation was not the best way to handle the strong, silent type. He just turned around and left when he didn't want to talk about something.

She ran upstairs to check on Riley and found him awake. She brought him down and fed him. Hungrily he ate three jars of baby food. Most babies would have been howling if they had been that hungry, but he had been patiently waiting in his crib.

She picked him up and hugged him, loving the way he nestled into her shoulder.

"You can ask for what you want, sweetheart. Believe me, you'll be happier in the long run if you learn to speak up."

She knew that from personal experience.

She put Riley down on the blanket on the floor and put the toys within his reach. He made no move for the toys, but he did watch her every move. She talked to him the whole time she scrubbed potatoes and took an inventory of the contents of the pantry.

"Canned vegetables. That's the best we can do. We should have stopped at the market."

She finished her preparation for dinner and scrubbed down the car seat, then folded the clean clothes and carried them and the baby upstairs.

She opened the second drawer of the chest and found it empty except for a facedown framed photo. She pulled it out of the drawer and turned it over. It was a picture of a man with two boys who looked to be about ten and twelve. The man looked like an older version of Griff, and except for the difference in their size, the boys looked almost exactly alike. This had to be Griff and his father and brother.

She studied the photo, trying to decide which boy was Griff. She guessed the bigger of the two boys. Although he was smiling, he had a more thoughtful, serious look than the younger boy, who mugged for the camera.

She started to set the photo on the dresser, then stopped, wondering why it had been in the drawer in the first place. It was the only personal item that hinted of family she had seen in the house, and it lay facedown in the drawer.

Suddenly she didn't feel comfortable leaving it out and returned it to its original spot. She laid the piles of clean clothes on top of the frame, pondering why it would be hidden away in a drawer.

It was part of Riley's past, this photo of his father and uncle and grandfather. Someday she hoped that it would mean something to Riley, that his father would warm up enough to tell his son family stories that would give the child a sense of his past.

She looked over at the little boy and wondered if she would have enough time to bring father and son together. She hoped so.

She missed her own father, even though she was still furious with him for all his manipulation in her life and furious with herself for letting him.

She repeated her new mantra. I live with courage. She would bring father and son together before she left.

Griff washed up at the bunkhouse and endured the teasing from his ranch hands about sprucing up before he went home to the little woman. Actually he was killing time, not wanting to face her.

She'd had a whole day to come up with more questions and demands, and no matter how pretty and sweet smelling she was, he was too tired to deal with her tonight.

He gave instruction to the two men on night duty, then headed to the house in the deepening twilight, his stomach growling to the accompaniment of his boots thumping against the dry ground.

The door from the back porch to the kitchen was open, and he could see her next to the stove. If she had fixed rabbit food for dinner again, he was going to make a beeline right back to the bunkhouse and eat with the men, no matter what amount of ribbing he took from his hands.

Climbing the back steps, he decided to let the men think he was interested in her. It would keep them from wasting time sniffing around the back door. This was not the kind of woman who was going to be interested in a ranch hand, even on a casual basis.

No way was she a casual woman. He didn't know her, but she didn't flirt and send signals in that direction.

He took off his jacket, then sat down on the bench just inside the porch door and pulled off his boots. The good smells coming from the kitchen put him in an optimistic frame of mind.

The porch looked all tidy, and the top of the freezer was cleared off. Hopefully she'd been busy enough today that she'd be too tired to hound him.

He got up and stretched his aching muscles, then paused in the kitchen door and watched Jolie, her back to him, at the stove. The baby must be asleep. He tamped down a twinge of guilt at the relief that he wouldn't have to see the kid.

It wasn't Riley's fault that he was a constant reminder of his wife's infidelity and his brother's betrayal.

The old radio on top of the refrigerator was on low and Garth Brooks was singing about having friends in low places. Jolie was swaying slowly to the music, her hips encased in a pair of fancy jeans that had never made contact with a saddle.

She bent over and pulled open the broiler and his mouth went dry. The woman had a very fine set of curves.

He came up behind her, his hands fairly itching. He hooked his thumbs in his belt loops and prayed for self-control. "That smells good."

She gasped and spun around, crashing into him with an elbow to his ribs.

"You scared me!"

He winced and grabbed her arms to steady her as she bounced off him.

"Sorry, I thought you heard me out on the porch." He had noticed she had a tendency to daydream and wondered what went on in her pretty little head.

She stepped back out of his grasp. Reluctantly he let her go, surprised how firm the muscles in her arms felt. She wasn't as fragile as she looked. But, damn, she still smelled good. Even better than the steak in the broiler.

She smiled up at him, looking more composed. "I was thinking about something. How do you like your steak?"

"Rare." And he liked his women pretty and slim and blond, just like her.

"Okay. Then dinner is ready." She grabbed a platter and opened the broiler again, forking two steaks onto it.

He took it out of her hands and set it next to a salad and a basket of bread. Now, this was the kind of meal he liked.

She carried a casserole of scalloped potatoes over, then went back to the stove for a bowl of green beans.

Griff forgot all about what the hands were eating in the bunkhouse and pulled a chair up to the table. Even Margie never managed a meal like this.

"Looks good."

"Thanks." She slipped into the chair across from him and cut a piece off one of the steaks, sliding it onto her plate.

Griff tore into his food and was having seconds when he realized with some relief that there had been no conversation at all. He didn't think of her as the quiet type, in fact she'd had her cute little nose in his business since he'd hired her.

He looked across the table at Jolie, and she smiled.

She didn't look angry. In his experience that was the one thing that might keep a woman from talking.

"Good dinner." He scooped more potatoes onto his plate.

"Thank you." She pushed a piece of steak around her plate. "May I ask you a question?"

He knew it had been too good to last. "What?"

"Would it be all right with you if I take the baby to the doctor?"

"Is he sick?" Hadn't they covered the doctor thing already?

"No, no," she said quickly.

He felt a spurt of relief that surprised him.

She put her fork down across her plate. "Do you know anything about his medical history?"

"How much history can a ten-month-old have?"

"I'm thinking of vaccinations, shots."

He vaccinated his calves. Made sense they did the same thing for babies. "I don't know."

She shifted uneasily in her seat, obviously uncomfortable, but she plowed right ahead. "Maybe you could contact your wife."

He stared at her until she started to squirm. The pain of an old familiar ache ate at him. "My wife is dead."

He watched the shock of his blunt words register on her expressive face, then embarrassment.

"I'm sorry. I…" She looked as if she was searching for something else to say.

He closed his eyes for a moment until the anger at Deirdre and Jake's irresponsible behavior flared. The betrayal he could understand. Deirdre had been a beautiful, enticing woman. There was no excuse for driving drunk.

When he looked at her again, all he saw was sympathy. He didn't correct her misreading of the situation.

He didn't plan to explain the whole sordid mess to her, either. Let her believe it was grief keeping him quiet.

"Thanks for dinner." He got up and left her sitting at the table, staring after him.

Chapter Five

The alarm jolted Jolie out of a dream that involved Griff and herself and a blanket in the bed of his truck. She put her hands to her hot cheeks. Her dreams weren't usually so, well, erotic.

She rolled to her side and slapped the button to silence the annoying beep, squinting at the time. Five o'clock.

For heaven's sake it was still dark outside. Groggy, she wondered why her alarm was set for the ungodly hour, then she remembered last night.

Miserable over her prying at dinner, last night Jolie lay in bed a long time thinking about Griff. Obviously, she'd opened a wound with her questions.

She thought about Griff's words and the look on his face as the meal ended, before he'd gotten up and walked out.

My wife is dead.

She'd decided to get up early and fix him breakfast and pack a lunch. She couldn't make the loss of his wife any easier, but she could see that he was taken care of.

Up until now she'd been going about getting father and son together all wrong. What was the old saying, she thought? You can catch more flies with honey than you could with vinegar. Maybe Griff had been staying away from the house because coming home was not that appealing to him.

She was going to change tactics.

He worked long hours. From what she'd noticed when she arose in the mornings, he left with only coffee in his stomach and didn't take a lunch. She thought of the salad she'd prepared the first night and the disappointed look on his face when he realized that was the whole meal.

Drowsily she decided she'd have to work on that. Surprisingly she found the thought of having him around more appealing. But, she reminded herself, it was all for Riley. She was doing this for the child.

Jolie rolled out of bed, pulled on her jeans and headed for the kitchen. She felt terrible to have misjudged him so badly. She had mistaken his surly reticence as... what? She pondered as she got eggs and milk out of the refrigerator. A part of his personality? Now she realized he was hiding his pain by being gruff and uncommunicative.

Understanding what had happened to him helped, but a few things still nagged at her. Obviously, Griff and his wife had been separated for a while, because he told her he knew little about Riley. And why would he act as if he didn't want to be involved with his son? If he was grieving over his wife, wouldn't he want to be close to the part of her she had left behind in his child?

She mixed up batter for pancakes and made a decision. She had already misjudged the situation so badly, she decided not to make any more assumptions when it came to Griff Price.

She'd heard him come in about midnight. Instead of being able to sleep once she knew he was home, she'd listened to the water running through the pipes in the wall beside her bed as he showered, and imagined what he looked like with water pouring over that big, long body.

No assumptions, she thought as she poured herself a cup of coffee, and no more fantasies.

Griff heard her in the kitchen as he came down the stairs. The smell of coffee and pancakes rose up to meet him. His mouth watered. How long had it been since he'd awakened to the smell of breakfast?

Since his dad died last year. In the last few years before his death his father's arthritis had become so bad he hadn't been able to spend a full day doing ranch work, but he had cooked every morning.

Griff missed those early mornings with his dad, the conversations about the ranch and even the silence when they ran out of things that needed to be said.

He rounded the door and there she was, in her fancy jeans and a butter-yellow sweater that clung softly and outlined the shape of her breasts. She put a platter of pancakes on the kitchen table, then looked up and smiled.

He suddenly felt breathless, as if someone had punched him in the gut. If he hadn't been sure he was awake he'd have pinched himself.

"Good morning." She greeted him cheerfully.

"Morning." What was she up to? When a woman did something nice like this she usually wanted something. "Where's the baby?"

"Still asleep. He usually sleeps until about seven."

She hadn't gotten up early because of the baby. His suspicion kicked into full gear as he pulled out one of the ladder-back chairs and sat down, taking note of the place mats and napkins. The syrup was in a little glass pitcher instead of the bottle, and there was a saucer under his cup of coffee.

Jolie had turned back to the stove and was pouring more batter onto the sizzling griddle.

He eyed her with wariness. What was going on here?

Then he remembered the conversation as supper ended last night and the impression he'd left her with concerning his grief for his dead wife.

He forked pancakes onto his plate and felt a little guilty, then he took a bite and decided if that's what it took for her to get up and cook for him he could handle a little guilt.

"This is really good. Thanks."

She'd moved to the counter beside the refrigerator and was busy pulling things out of the fridge. She looked over her shoulder and smiled at him again. "You're welcome."

She had a great smile. It made her look less aloof and more approachable. He'd been thinking a lot about approaching her. Especially in the middle of the night when he woke up in a sweat after some fine dreams about her.

"Aren't you going to eat?" he asked, admiring the way her jeans fitted snugly over her butt. Day and night her sweet little body was driving him nuts.

"Later. My stomach wakes up about nine."

Sure it did. Rich girls could have breakfast any time they wanted. He finished up the last bite of pancake and sighed with pleasure. He liked starting work on a full stomach. Somehow it made his outlook on the whole day better.

He looked up, and she was standing next to his chair, paper and pen in hand.

"I need you to do something."

Oh, boy. He knew there would be a payoff. "What?"

"I need your permission to take Riley to the doctor. If there were ever an emergency, I couldn't make any decisions without your authorization."

That made sense. He took the pen and paper from her and wrote out his permission, then signed it.

Jolie heard him stand up. Getting him to sign had been easier than she thought.

She felt guilty not telling him she intended to take Riley to a doctor, but until she had a professional opinion, she didn't want to bring up her suspicions that something was wrong with the baby.

Hurriedly she finished wrapping his sandwiches. This was not a man who hung around for idle conversation.

She turned quickly to tell him to wait and found she was inches from his large warm body.

Without saying a word he slid his arm around her waist. Startled, she took a quick step back and found herself pinned between the counter and the cowboy. He made no move to step back.

Senses reeling, she was immediately aware of two things. He smelled of pancake syrup and soap, and her breasts were up against his chest.

"I, uh, didn't want you to leave without your lunch." Her voice sounded a little breathless, as if she had just taken several flights of stairs.

He grinned down at her. "You fixed me lunch, too?"

"Uh, yes. You work so hard and I…" Whatever she

had been going to say slipped right out of her mind. He was staring at her mouth.

"Funny, all I can think about now is dessert." He leaned into her a little more.

The edge of the counter pressed into her back as he reached up and tugged gently on her hair until her head tipped back. He lowered his face to hers and brushed his lips across her mouth, exploring the texture and shape of her lips.

He drew back for just a moment, making her want to whimper, and gave her a long, smoldering look. Then he lowered his head again and kissed her hard and long.

When they finally came up for air Jolie realized he had turned her until he was leaning against the counter. She was plastered full against him, breasts to knees, with her arms around his neck. His hands were cupping her bottom, pulling her up against the obvious bulge in his jeans.

Totally befuddled, Jolie untangled her arms and pushed herself away. She felt giddy and shaky. Perhaps the nickname Wild Man wasn't as unbelievable as she had thought.

He grinned again. "Thanks for breakfast."

"You're welcome," she said politely, then realized she sounded like a fool.

She gestured vaguely at the sandwiches. One of them was as flat as the pancakes she'd just served. It must have gotten squashed when they were…what were they doing anyway?

As good as the kiss had felt, somewhere in the back of her flustered mind she knew it hadn't been a good idea.

"Don't forget your…" She couldn't seem to come up with the name for the midday meal.

"Gotta go." He scooped up the sandwiches and disappeared out the back door.

Jolie made her way to a kitchen chair and sat down to get her wits about her.

She took a couple of deep breaths and tried to pull herself together. Letting him kiss her had probably been a huge mistake.

But it didn't feel like a mistake.

And that, she realized, was the danger.

Then she decided she was being silly. One kiss didn't mean anything. She was blowing things out of proportion.

She was just a little unsure of herself when it came to men after being dumped on her wedding day, and his attention was flattering, nothing more.

Sure, said a little voice in her head. Did Charles ever make your brain go numb when he kissed you?

Not even once, she thought and rubbed her fingers across her mouth. She glanced at the clock and realized she'd been sitting and staring into space for quite a while.

She got to her feet, reassured when her legs seemed to have regained their strength, and headed up the stairs.

Riley was awake in his crib, sitting in a corner quietly waiting for her.

She picked him up and nuzzled his neck. "You know, buddy, it's okay to holler when you want to get up. Babies do it all the time."

She changed him and carried him downstairs. Since there was no high chair, Jolie put him on a kitchen chair and tied a dish towel around him to hold him there. Not that he made any effort to move, but she didn't want to take the chance of him pitching onto the floor.

Just as she finished feeding him, the phone rang. Jolie

picked up the receiver of the old wall phone. "Hello, Circle P."

"Jolie? It's Aunt Rosie. *What* is a Circle P? You aren't working in one of those dreadful convenience stores are you?"

Jolie smothered a laugh. "No, Aunt Rosie. The Circle P is a ranch."

"I just got home and got your message. I spoke to that wretched brother of mine. He told me he cancelled your credit cards."

She felt an absurd need to defend her father. "Well, he didn't want me to drive cross country."

Rosie went on with her tirade. "He told me under no circumstances was I to help you. He thinks he can force you to come home by cutting you off."

"I know, but—"

"Don't you even think about buckling under to that kind of intimidation! I just wired money to you care of Western Union in Billings."

Jolie had always been able to count on her Aunt Rosie. "Thank you."

"And I want you to come here as soon as your car is repaired."

"I will. Rosie, did you tell Daddy where I was?"

"Of course not. He'd come and drag you back by your hair. I told him you were safe. You are safe, aren't you, dear?"

Jolie thought about Griff's kiss. That depended on what Aunt Rosie meant by safe.

"Yes, I'm safe. The ranch is wonderful, and I'll stay here until the car is ready. I'll call you when I'm on my way to New York."

Jolie didn't want to explain about Griff and Riley,

which was strange because she told Aunt Rosie everything.

"You enjoy your resort and call me if you need more money."

"I will. Thanks again Aunt Rosie." She'd explain to her aunt later that the Circle P was far from a resort.

She hung up the phone and went to Riley and untied him. She picked him up, held him out with her arms extended and spun around. "Bless Aunt Rosie!"

The baby smiled and squealed in delight. It was the first sound Jolie had ever heard him make. She hugged him. Now she wouldn't have to worry about money to pay for the doctor.

"Riley, we're going into town and we're going to celebrate. A high chair for you and some clothes for me." She couldn't very well do housework and take care of a baby in dry-clean-only designer clothes.

She looked in the yellow pages, picked out the pediatrician with the most foreign-sounding name, and made an appointment for later in the morning.

She headed toward town in Griff's truck, still feeling as if she were driving an eighteen-wheeler. What a day this was shaping up to be. Riley had responded to her, Aunt Rosie had come through with some money, and Griff....

The thought of his kiss this morning brought a rush of warmth. He was a mighty fine kisser, but she suspected he'd kissed her just because she was...well, there.

After all, he'd just lost his wife and was still grieving for her. Jolie had gotten in his way at a moment when he was feeling...what?

Whatever it was, she thought, as she pulled up and parked in front of the Western Union office, she wasn't going to take it seriously.

For heaven's sake, she still hadn't figured out why Charles had dumped her. He hadn't had the nerve to tell her to her face, but instead sent her a message through his sister, who was one of her bridesmaids.

It was very humiliating to be dumped as you stood in the back of the church with the wedding march playing, but even more so to be dumped through a third party.

None of that changed the fact that Griff was a mighty fine kisser, she thought as she hauled the baby out of the car seat.

She picked up the money, more than enough to last her until she got to Aunt Rosie's, and stuffed the cash into her pocket, then put the baby back in the truck and headed to the doctor's office.

After a short wait while she filled out paperwork, they were ushered into the exam room. She removed his clothes and blew a raspberry on his bare tummy and then laughed at his look of surprise.

The nurse came in and weighed him.

"Fifteen pounds, even."

The doctor arrived and introduced herself, then checked Riley from head to toe.

"He's a bit underweight for his height. How's his appetite?"

"He's a good eater." She outlined his daily diet.

The doctor sat him up. "Well, sometimes at this age they are so active you can't get enough food in them."

"I wanted to talk to you about that." Jolie explained as much of the situation as she knew, then expressed her concerns over how quiet he was.

The doctor picked Riley up and he looked over at Jolie. "How long have you been taking care of him?"

"Just a few days."

The doctor consulted her chart and frowned. "No medical history?"

"No. His father just got custody of him. I don't know exactly what happened, but I gather there was very little communication between the father and mother, then the mother died suddenly."

"Give him as much attention as you can. Interactive games, peek-a-boo, that kind of thing. He's suffered an emotional trauma, but he should start to respond."

Relieved, Jolie took him from the doctor. "I've already seen a bit of improvement." She didn't mention Griff's distance to the child. That was something she intended to work on.

"Well, in a case like this when we don't have a history, we like to give all the vaccinations."

"What if he's had his shots? Won't it be dangerous to have them again?"

"No. The danger is leaving a child unvaccinated. Bring him back in a month and we'll see how he's doing. The nurse will be in to give him his injections."

"All right." The new nanny would be bringing him back, she thought with a pang. "Thank you."

He howled as the nurse gave him two shots, and Jolie felt awful as she fought back tears.

As soon as the nurse was finished, Jolie scooped Riley up and hugged him, crooning soothing words as she patted his back.

The nurse smiled. "Vaccinations always hurt the mom more than the baby. You watch, he'll recover before you do."

She gathered up the syringes and left the room, then stuck her head back in through the door. "He may get fussy later. Just give him a dose of liquid Tylenol."

Riley quieted down and Jolie stood there holding him

as he sniffled against her shoulder. The nurse thought she was his mom. With a pang she realized how much she wished she was. She sat him down on the exam table and dressed him.

When she'd agreed to marry Charles, she knew she wasn't madly in love with him, but she was in love with the idea of having a home and children.

"You know, buddy," she said to Riley as she snapped the fastener on his overalls, "I think we need to go have lunch before we shop. What do you think?"

Riley hiccuped and held out his arms, and Jolie's heart melted as she gathered up his small body and hugged him.

Chapter Six

Jolie whistled as she drove back to the ranch, trying not to think about the way Griff had kissed her this morning. She ran her tongue over her bottom lip. It was like trying to not breathe all day.

She forced her thoughts to the contents of the cab. Bags of groceries and clothes filled the floor at Riley's feet. Clothes she had bought for herself at a discount store. Jeans and T-shirts and sweatshirts. And canvas shoes. And in the truck bed a used high chair from the resale shop.

She'd never worn anything but designer clothes, but then, she'd never worked on a ranch.

She laughed out loud thinking of what her father, a terrible snob who would only buy the best, would say if he knew where she'd been shopping. He'd probably want to have her committed.

She hummed along with the radio, listening to a song that admonished the listener to "stand by your man."

As soon as she pulled up to the house, cowboy Chris was there to help her unload.

She eyed him as she slid from the high seat of the truck. "If you work all night, when do you sleep?"

He grinned at her. "Oh, I get enough." He gave her a wink.

She turned away to get the sleeping baby, aware of the blatant flirting. She decided to ignore the innuendo and take advantage of his help.

"If you'd take the high chair around the side and leave it on the cement slab where the hose is, I'd appreciate it."

"Sure thing."

She carried Riley up to his bed. The poor child was worn out from his visit to the doctor and their busy trip to town.

She needed to run her new clothes through the washer before she wore them, but didn't have nearly enough for a full load. Riley's hamper was nearly empty, but Griff must have things that needed washing.

His bedroom door was open and she hesitated on the threshold. His room was a reflection of the man. Plain solid furniture and no personal belongings that would give anyone a hint as to who occupied the room.

Hesitantly she entered and found a wash basket full of dirty clothes in his closet. Jeans, flannel shirts, and plain white underwear.

Briefs.

She would have figured him for briefs.

If she was the kind of woman who guessed that sort of thing.

The scent of him wafted up from the dirty clothes. Heaven help her, even his dirty clothes were sexy.

"Get a grip on yourself, Jolie," she muttered as she hoisted the laundry basket against her hip.

But the spicy scent of his soap brought back this morning's kiss, and she went warm and breathless all over again.

Until this minute she didn't remember noticing his scent this morning, but then she probably wouldn't have noticed a bomb going off, either.

When she got back downstairs all her purchases were on the kitchen table and the truck was gone.

She had been so busy mooning over Griff's dirty laundry she hadn't had the manners to thank Chris for his help.

She really did need to get a grip.

Griff knocked off work a little early. The streak of bad luck seemed to be over, and things around the ranch were finally under control. The fences were mended and so was the main water tank, and the windmill pump in the south pasture where he kept the bull was up and running.

He had a bunch of paperwork to catch up on, not to mention some reading he had been trying to get to for weeks.

He headed toward the back of the house. No matter how many reasons he gave himself that he was coming back early, he knew the real reason was a pretty little blonde.

He might work for a while, then just get himself a beer and sit in the kitchen and watch her fix dinner, because, Lord, he liked to watch the woman move.

That kiss this morning had about curled the soles off his boots. And he hadn't been the only one. He doubted she could have told him her name when he let go of her.

Those big brown eyes of hers had an unfocused look that he found very sexy. He smiled smugly at the thought that he had put that look there and let himself relive the feel of her. He wanted her. Bad.

They were two consenting adults. There was no reason they couldn't—his musings were cut off by a scream that sounded like a dying rabbit.

He raced around the side of the house and spotted Jolie standing on the old outside shower slab, a rusty garden hoe raised in one hand. She looked like an avenging angel brandishing a sword.

She was gearing up for another scream when he got to her.

"Whoa, sweetheart. What happened?" With one hand on her shoulder he pulled the hoe out of her trembling fingers and leaned it against the house.

"I...I..."

"Okay, take a deep breath." She was shaking and her breath chugged in and out like an old steam engine.

She pointed at the dirt beside the slab. "A...a snake."

He caught her as her knees buckled and hauled her up against his chest, where she vibrated like a buzz saw.

He looked down to where she had pointed. She had indeed killed a snake. A common garden snake. Griff guessed it had been about three feet long, but now the hapless serpent was neatly sliced into at least a dozen three-inch segments.

He swallowed a laugh. "Well sweetheart, looks like you conquered the viper."

She had stopped shaking so he let her take a step away from him.

She looked down. "Is it dead?"

He knelt down and studied the snake, averting his head because he didn't want her to see the smile he couldn't seem to wipe off his face. "I think that's a pretty safe assumption."

Just as he got ahold of himself and straightened up, Chris and Lem came barreling around the house and skidded to a halt just short of the cement.

Chris looked from Jolie to Griff. "You two okay? We were working on the thresher and thought we heard a scream."

Griff pointed to the snake. "We're fine. Jolie just made us all safer by killing off that snake."

Jolie nodded and started to babble. "I came out to scrub down the high chair and reached for the hose and there it was, just right there beside the pipe and...and..."

She was starting to do that fast breathing thing again, and she looked a mite pale.

Griff took her by the arm and led her over to an old plastic chair in the shade of a tree. "Sit down, sweetheart, and put your head down for a minute."

He wrapped his hand around the back of her warm, smooth neck and pushed her head down gently. "Take a couple of deep breaths."

Her hair slid like warm silk over his wrist. If his men hadn't been there he would have pulled her up and into his arms and tried a little mouth-to-mouth.

He looked over at Chris and Lem as they stared down at the dead snake. He heard one of the men mutter something, then a snort of muffled laughter. Then they both broke loose, hooting and howling. Lem came up for air first, using his sleeve to wipe the tears off his face.

Before he could signal his hands to shut up, Jolie shook off Griff and sat up in the chair, glaring at Chris and Lem.

"Are you laughing at me?" she asked, clearly offended.

"No ma'am," Chris managed to get out before he started snorting again.

Griff could see how embarrassed Jolie was by the pink of her cheeks. "Lem, you and Chris get on back to what you were doing."

"Sure, boss. Thresher's almost fixed." They both turned to leave.

Chris looked over his shoulder at the snake and muttered something to Lem that started them laughing all over again.

Jolie got up out of her chair, her back as stiff as a poker. "I have things to do, too."

Griff watched her disappear around the side of the house, then headed after Lem and Chris to get a shovel. He couldn't resist the urge to look at the snake when he passed by.

Jolie certainly had done a thorough job on the poor creature. He shook his head. The city girl might be easy on the eyes, but she sure didn't belong here in Montana.

Jolie stood on the enclosed porch and watched the rain coming down in sheets. She was used to rain, having been raised in Seattle, but she'd come to love the sunshine and big blue skies of Montana.

It was just as well she had to stay in, she thought with a sigh, because after the incident with the snake yesterday she certainly wasn't going to go outside where she might run into Chris or any of the other hands. No doubt she had been the laughingstock of the bunkhouse last night.

"Riley," she said as she shifted the child on her hip, "I might have overreacted a bit, but it was not a good reason to make fun of me. It's not polite to make fun of people.''

Jolie moved into the living room. Griff had not laughed at her, but she could tell it had been a struggle for him.

She hated the idea she might be the topic of laughter in the bunkhouse, but the thought that Griff might think she was silly or stupid was too hard to bear. She decided to keep busy and not think about it at all.

Then there was the kiss. What a kiss. She wasn't going to think about that, either.

She put Riley down on the living room floor and checked the book on child development she'd picked up in Billings the day before, turning to the section on the ten-month-old baby. She read with dismay all the things a ten-month-old should be able to do.

Riley did none of them. No crawling or clapping or waving bye-bye. He didn't hold a toy in one hand, let alone two, and he made no attempt to pull himself up on furniture.

Well what was she going to do? Sit here feeling bad about the child's lack of development or do something about it?

Jolie repeated her mantra to herself. I live with courage.

If she was going to do more than just spout the words, she would have to get going.

She went and gathered up a few toys, then got down on the floor with Riley and sat facing him, her legs crossed.

"Riley, we're going to play. I have a suspicion that no one ever played with you."

The baby watched her intently, his big blue eyes steady on her face.

"We're going to do this every day. You're going to baby school until you catch up."

Jolie proceeded to develop a curriculum to help him catch up on the basic idea of play. Riley watched her stack blocks and line up toys. He didn't participate, but seemed to enjoy the interaction.

She became so engrossed in their play she lost track of the time.

Around noon Griff came into the porch and peeled off his slicker and boots, then put on a pair of sneakers. He was starving, and felt disappointed when he realized Jolie wasn't in the kitchen and there was no sign of lunch. He was getting used to her taking care of his meals.

He could hear Jolie's voice, but he couldn't hear what she was saying. He followed the sound and discovered Jolie and the kid on the floor in the living room. They were both on their hands and knees. Her sleek blond hair fell over her face like a curtain, and she didn't know he was there.

What the hell was she up to? His gaze shifted to his nephew.

He got a knot in his gut every time he looked at the kid. How long until he got past the sense of betrayal he felt every time he saw Riley? He pushed the thought aside.

He watched with growing curiosity as he listened to what she was saying.

"You just move one hand, then one knee. Then you do the same with the other hand and knee."

Griff leaned against the doorjamb and watched as she demonstrated her crawling technique to the kid, who, in Griff's opinion, looked a little puzzled.

"Don't they usually learn that by themselves?"

Jolie's head whipped around as he spoke, then she scrambled to her feet and smoothed her palms down the front of her jeans.

"Well, yes, they usually do, but I think Riley needs a little help."

Griff shrugged. He really didn't care, but at least she was talking to him. She'd acted so embarrassed over the snake yesterday she'd been avoiding him.

"Any chance of you fixing lunch?"

She glanced at the clock over the mantle. "Oh, I didn't realize it had gotten so late. I'll fix you something quick so you can go back to work."

"No big hurry. It's too wet out there to get anything done. I'm taking a couple of hours off." He picked up the remote control and flipped on the TV.

The screen flickered on, and he punched the button until he found the football game he was looking for.

"Good. You work too hard." She bent over and scooped the kid off the floor.

What a city girl. That comment showed how much she knew about ranching. It was nothing but hard work. He settled down onto the sofa and put his feet up on the coffee table.

Jolie walked over to the couch and set the kid right next to him. "You can keep an eye on him while I fix you lunch."

She turned and left the room so quickly he didn't get over the surprise before she was gone.

He was about to holler for her when he looked down and saw Riley was staring up at him, his little chin quivering. If he yelled the kid would probably bust out in a full-blown wail.

He started to get up and tell her to come and get the

boy, but he didn't know if he could just leave the kid sitting alone on the sofa.

Damn it all, anyway. This was why he had hired her, so she could take care of the kid. Every time he looked at him all he could see was betrayal.

Griff didn't want to feel the warm weight of him as he leaned against his side. He didn't want to look at his eyes that reminded him so much of his brother.

"Jolie, get in here," He hollered.

He had called it right. The kid started to wail.

Jolie came flying out of the kitchen still holding a dripping tomato. "What's the matter?"

Griff bolted off the couch and headed for the front door. "I gotta go." He opened the front door and stepped out into the pouring rain and mud of the yard, feeling like seven kinds of fool.

Jolie slipped the tomato into her apron pocket, picked up Riley and held him against her shoulder, where he quieted almost immediately. She stared at the front door.

"What happened?" She asked as she rubbed his back. "Did he scare you with all that yelling?"

The foolish man had gone out into the rain without a jacket or even his hat. What in the world had gotten into him?

She put Riley in the high chair and put a handful of cereal on the tray, then went back to preparing lunch and pondering Griff's strange behavior.

She hadn't heard his cell phone ring. Had he suddenly thought of something he needed to do?

She finished making the sandwiches and heating the soup, listening for him to return. She fed Riley and took him upstairs for his nap. Griff still hadn't returned.

Finally Jolie sat down to eat. As she was finishing her sandwich, she heard Griff come in the back porch.

She got up and opened the kitchen door leading to the porch just as Griff pulled off a soaking wet T-shirt. He stood by the washer in nothing but his dripping wet jeans.

Her mouth went dry, and she couldn't tear her eyes away. The man was truly beautiful. Muscular and honed, he looked like an underwear model in *GQ*.

She looked up at his face and saw that he had caught her staring. She expected a teasing smile, but instead he had a very hard expression.

"What happened?"

He quirked an eyebrow at her as if he didn't know what she was talking about. "When?"

"About a half hour ago when you left as if the house was on fire, that's when!" How obtuse could the man be?

"Oh, that. Nothing happened. I'm dripping all over the floor."

Indeed there was a growing puddle around his big bare feet. She couldn't have cared less. Something very weird was going on here.

"We need to talk."

He stared at her intently for a moment. "Yeah, we do. As soon as I go get some dry clothes." He sounded angry.

Something must have happened. "There's a load in the dryer."

He began to unfasten his jeans, and Jolie turned quickly and returned to the kitchen. If she saw any more of him she'd turn into a stuttering idiot.

She reheated his soup in the microwave and unwrapped his sandwich. He came into the kitchen and sat down at the table.

Jolie took the chair opposite him. He ate the way he

did everything else, but now his calm efficiency didn't hide the tension in his broad shoulders.

She held her tongue. There was no point in starting the conversation until he was finished. He didn't talk while he ate.

He polished off the last of the soup and pushed his bowl aside, then gave her a hard look.

"I hired you to take care of the kid, and that's what I expect you to do."

"I don't understand." Taking care of Riley is what she had been doing twenty-four hours a day since she got here.

"I don't want you to dump him on me."

Dump him? Is that why he had yelled for her loud enough to make the baby cry and bolted out of the house into the pouring rain?

"You were watching TV. I thought you would enjoy a little time with your son." She was trying very hard to control her temper. How dare he?

He clutched the edge of the table until his knuckles were white. He opened his mouth, then seemed to think better of what he was about to say.

Jolie plunged right in with things she had wanted to say since she arrived. "You need the interaction and so does Riley. You're hardly ever home when he's awake. How are you going to get to know your own child if you don't spend time with him?"

He stood up so abruptly his chair skidded back across the linoleum.

"He's—not—my—child!"

Jolie could only stare at him. What was he talking about? Did he think his wife had had another man's child and foisted it off on Griff? Couldn't he see the resemblance?

"What do you mean he's not your child? He looks just like you!"

"No. He looks just like my brother." His voice was oddly flat and toneless.

Jolie thought of the framed photo she had found upstairs in Riley's dresser of the two boys, almost identical in looks.

"He's your nephew." That didn't explain the animosity. Then a thought occurred to Jolie. "Riley's mother is…"

Griff made a choking sound. "Was. My wife."

All of a sudden Jolie realized what had happened.

Griff's wife and his brother had had an affair.

At least now she could understand why Riley made Griff so uncomfortable.

She didn't want to cause him further pain, but she had to know, for Riley.

Gently she asked, "Is your brother dead, too?"

Looking incredibly weary, Griff ran his hand down his face. "Yeah. They were out celebrating. Jake won a rodeo down in Oklahoma. They got drunk. He hit a telephone pole going over a hundred. They were both killed instantly."

Jolie was horrified. "Was Riley with them?"

"No. They left him with a sitter in a motel. When they didn't come back she called child services. It took them six weeks to call me." Griff sat down as if he was too tired to stand anymore.

Poor Riley. Poor Griff. Every time he looked at the baby he must think of his wife's infidelity and his brother's betrayal.

Would he ever be able to get past what had happened and parent this child? Jolie had her doubts.

Now so many things that had troubled her made sense.

Like Griff's reluctance to interact with Riley. And the nickname Wild Man had belonged to Griff's brother.

Silently she cursed them for what they had done to Griff and to their child.

"I know it must have been terrible for you when your wife and brother betrayed you, but you can't blame Riley."

He looked at her, surprise written all over his face. "I don't blame the kid."

"But you can't stand to be in the same room with him."

Griff didn't deny that.

"Do you think you can get past what happened?" He had to, for Riley and for himself.

Griff shook his head, then rubbed his palms down his face. He folded his hands under his chin, elbows on the table.

"Honestly? I don't know."

"Would you consider giving him up for adoption?" Jolie would take him in a heartbeat if Griff said yes.

He looked at Jolie as if she was crazy. "Of course not. He's family."

In spite of her sympathy for him her temper flashed. "So, let me get this straight. You won't have anything to do with him, but you won't give him up. You want him in your house but not your life. You want to hire someone to raise him."

"That's not the way it is." Griff protested.

Jolie could tell he was getting ready to bolt. "That's *exactly* the way it is, and you know it!" she said, furious at his stubborn attitude.

He didn't want to see what was perfectly clear. No matter how much he'd been hurt, a child's well-being was at stake.

He threw his napkin down and stood up. "You don't know what the hell you're talking about!"

"You don't want to face the truth, and because of that a child is suffering."

Griff got up and slammed out the back door without saying another word.

She watched him go. The man sure was good at leaving. But she knew him well enough by now to know he would always come back.

She would just take her comfort in that.

Chapter Seven

Jolie held dinner for him. She'd gotten over her anger almost before he'd left. The heart-wrenching mixture of pain and grief she saw in Griff when he'd told her about how he'd come to have Riley had stayed with her all afternoon.

She watched him come across the yard. Even tired and bedraggled, he looked delicious.

By now she knew his routine. He came in through the back porch, sat on the bench and removed his muddy boots. Then he changed his shirt. When she did laundry she had taken to hanging a clean shirt on a nail by the dryer.

He washed up in the tub beside the dryer and made his way into the kitchen with a body language that indicated he wasn't at all sure how he would be received.

Jolie got up from the table as he entered the kitchen.

"Jolie, I'm sorry for what happened this afternoon. I just...I don't know..." He ran his hands through his hair as his voice trailed off.

She studied him for a moment, took a deep breath, then faced the problem head-on. "You think of what your wife and brother did every time you look at Riley, don't you?"

"Yeah, I do."

Choking back tears she said, "You can't take it out on Riley. It isn't his fault."

Griff just stood there, not saying a word.

Jolie got a grip on her emotions and plowed on while she still had the courage. She repeated her earlier question. "Would you consider putting him up for adoption?"

"No! He's family. I'll give him a home."

She reached out and put her hand on his arm. "And ignore him for the next twenty years? He needs a parent."

Griff put his big hand over hers. "He's got you to take care of him."

She pulled back. "I'm temporary."

Oh, how it hurt to say that, more than she would have guessed.

From the look on his face he'd lost track of that little fact. "Then I'll hire someone else."

"They'll be temporary, too." She tried to hold on to her emotions, but tears were close to the surface again. "Can't you see he needs love?"

Griff's shoulders sagged. "I don't know if I can come to love him."

She said gently, "Let's start by working on keeping you both in the same room. Try to see him for who he is."

Griff stared at her for a moment, then nodded.

Jolie recognized a milestone when she saw one, but curbed her reaction. Matter-of-factly she asked, "Can you come in a little earlier tomorrow? We'll do this together. I'll stay with you and if it gets too bad, you can leave. Just a few minutes at first, okay?"

He looked skeptical. "I suppose."

"It'll be okay. I promise." She drew him in for a quick hug, then let go because it felt so good to have him in her arms.

He lowered his big frame into the kitchen chair and leaned back with a sigh as she slid a big bowl of beef stew and a basket of biscuits in front of him.

He looked up and gave her a tired smile. "Thanks. This smells great."

Jolie went to the sink to scrub the pots and pans, watching him as he worked his way through the huge bowl of stew. Perhaps some of the other men on the ranch could interact with the baby, too. Help Riley become more social. Chris, despite his teasing over the snake incident, seemed like a nice person.

If she could get Griff to work as hard on a relationship with Riley as he did with his cows, things would work out all right.

She dried the last pot then walked to him and laid her hand on his broad shoulder. She felt the warm, hard muscle flex ever so slightly and felt an answering quiver in her own body. Quickly she removed her hand. The attraction was a complication she didn't need.

"I know how hard you work to keep your ranch running, but you won't be sorry you took the time for Riley. I promise."

He glanced up at her and neither agreed or disagreed. "I'll give it a try. That's all I can promise."

She had already discovered he was a man of his word, and she could be stubborn, so between them they would get Riley squared away.

* * *

Jolie leaned against the washer, waiting for the cycle to end, and stared out into the yard, deep in thought. Riley had started to crawl today. Once he discovered he could get around, he had taken off like a rocket every time she put him down.

She was elated with his progress, but it did have its drawbacks. Her lower back ached from scooping him up and carrying him around. Although he had nearly fallen asleep in his lunch, he had fought going to bed for the first time.

She smiled as she remembered the indignant yelp upon being put in his crib. Every show of emotion was precious to her.

The ringing telephone made her jump.

She answered. "Circle P."

"Ms. Carleton?"

"Yes."

"This is the mechanic over at Winslow's Garage. Your car is ready."

The car might be ready, but she wasn't. She still had so much to do here. "I thought it was going to take another week."

"Nope. Ready to go."

"Thank you. I'll get someone to drive me in." He hung up before she finished her sentence. A real social guy, that mechanic, she thought with a smile.

As she tossed the wet jeans and T-shirts from the washer to the dryer, she thought how her life was as tangled with Griff and Riley as the clothes she was throwing in.

Would she be able to fold her life into a neat pile, separate from theirs, when she left?

She doubted it.

Her visit to Aunt Rosie could wait, and even when she got home to Seattle, there was nothing important waiting for her. She had agreed to help with the big charity ball in the spring, but there were plenty of other women on the committee.

Her hands stilled on the top of the dryer. Her life since she graduated from college had been Junior League projects, charity projects and trips.

Not an empty life, exactly, but certainly not full of challenge. She'd been just comfortably floating along, waiting to get married. And if Charles hadn't changed his mind, she'd still have the same life, only now it would contain a husband and a home.

The whole picture she conjured up depressed her. A little voice nagged at her, asking her what she was going to do about it?

She was going to live with courage and find a job as soon as she returned to Seattle from Rosie's. She realized now she'd *had* to run from her father, because two weeks ago she didn't have the courage to stand up to him.

Thinking back, Jolie hardly recognized the girl who had run from Seattle. That made her proud and more than a little scared. She was changing, but she wasn't sure who she was going to end up being.

One thing for sure, she wanted to put her degree in child development to use. Working with Riley had been the most satisfying thing she'd ever done.

In the future she would guard against getting so involved. The thought of having to leave Riley made her want to cry. She would have to toughen up and not become so attached. She could do that. It was just that Riley had sneaked up on her. She hadn't been expecting the situation.

The sound of frantic bellowing interrupted her thoughts. She looked up to see a huge red cow wander into the yard, bawling its head off.

Darn steak-on-the-hoof was going to wake up Riley. Jolie grabbed a dish towel from the top of the dryer and ran out the back door.

"Shoo! Quiet!" She waved the towel in the startled cow's face.

The huge bovine shook her head, the whites of her eyes showing.

Jolie stopped waving the towel and took a step backward. She had assumed this was a cow, but maybe she had made a major mistake and she was standing out here in the yard waving a towel in front of a bull.

She took another step back. From where she was she couldn't see the underside of the animal. Even if she could, she wasn't sure she would be able to tell a male from a female.

Just as she was considering trying to outrun the beast and make it to the back door, the animal stopped bawling and sank down on its knees then settled onto the ground, sides heaving.

Chris and Lem came around the side of the house carrying a tool box and some lengths of board. She hadn't seen either of them since that incident with the snake.

Chris looked at her, then at the cow, and back to the towel in her hand. He tipped his hat.

"Afternoon, ma'am."

Jolie nodded at him, then pointed at the animal. "Is that a bull?"

Chris, his lips twitching as if he had some kind of nervous condition, looked down at the animal on the ground, whose sides were now heaving in a very alarming way.

"No, ma'am. That's a cow."

She saw movement out of the corner of her eye and spotted Griff headed toward them.

Jolie turned her attention back to Chris. "What is she doing?"

"I think it would be safe to say she's calving."

Appalled, Jolie looked from the cow to the cowboy. "You mean she's having a baby? Right now? Here in the yard?"

Lem nodded. "Yes, ma'am. Appears so."

Panicked, Jolie couldn't believe how calm the men were. Griff walked up to the three of them and glanced down at the cow.

Jolie grabbed his sleeve. "What should we do?"

Griff looked at her intently, a slight smile on his beautiful lips. "Boil water and tear up your petticoat for bandages."

Jolie spun around toward the house to follow his directions, and he caught her by the arm as his words sunk in.

"Whoa. I was kidding."

He turned back to Lem but still held her arm in his big warm hand. "Isn't this the same one that had her last calf right outside the cookshack?"

"Yeah, boss. She must like company."

"Well, you two get to work and I'll see about her."

As his men turned toward the porch he dropped his hand. Jolie didn't miss the proprietary way he'd held on to her in front of his men. To her surprise she liked the feeling of belonging to him.

The cow's sides were heaving rhythmically now.

"Don't they usually do this in the spring?" Jolie eyed her with some hesitance.

"Usually. But we always have some winter calves. This old girl just loves to be different."

Griff watched the cow for a moment, then turned to Jolie. "Any chance I can get some lunch?"

Apparently, he was satisfied the cow was okay. Jolie had her doubts, but Griff would know if they had time to eat, wouldn't he?

"Sandwiches?" Jolie hadn't eaten yet, either.

"Fine."

She gestured to the cow. "How much longer will this take?" She wasn't going to be able to relax until she knew the beast was all right.

Griff walked around to the animal's hindquarters and waited until she had another contraction. "Not long now. Come here."

Jolie came to stand beside him. The cow shifted her position and with another huge heave of her sides, the calf slipped from her body, all spindly legs and quivering body.

Jolie stood transfixed as the mother cow struggled to her feet and calmly began to take care of her baby.

"Oh, my." She breathed, overcome by the suddenness of the birth and the beauty of a new life slipping into the world.

Gently Griff tugged the dish towel out of her hand and used a corner to wipe her face.

She didn't even realize she was crying.

"Pretty special?"

"Oh, yes. I've never seen anything like it."

"Come spring, it will happen hundreds of times a day." He turned her toward the house.

Jolie looked back over her shoulder. Come spring she wouldn't be here.

She felt a sudden longing for all the things she would miss about Montana, and the big cowboy walking toward the back door was at the top of the list.

Someone knocked on the back door just as she finished feeding the baby his breakfast.

She opened the door to a blast of cold air and found Chris on the back porch.

"Lem and me is going to town for supplies. I wondered if you needed anything."

She had so much to do this morning it would be great if he could save her a trip to town. "Oh, yes. My car is finished. Could one of you drive it back?"

"Sure."

"It's at Winslow's Garage. Do you know where that is?"

"Across the street from the diner?"

She nodded. "I'll call and let them know you're picking it up. I really appreciate this."

"No problem." He tipped his hat and took the porch steps two at a time.

She carried Riley to the living room for their morning session. He was making nice progress. Now she needed to ease Griff into the mix and make sure he was comfortable with the baby.

Then…she could leave. Her car was repaired and she had money. There was no real reason for her to stay.

As she handed Riley blocks and encouraged him to stack them, she thought about the next few days. She'd have to talk to Griff about finding a new nanny for Riley.

The thought of someone else taking care of the baby

made her heart ache, but he wasn't her child. Her stay here had always been a temporary thing.

Eyes tearing, she watched Riley manage to stack three blocks. Then he crowed and knocked the stack over.

"Good job, buddy!" Jolie wiped a tear from her cheek and clapped, handing him the blocks again.

She thought of Griff's kiss and his casual way of touching her. She liked the feel of his hands on her too much.

She needed to keep her distance until she left. They wanted very different things. As it stood now he'd be hard to get over. If she let the heat between them get out of hand, she wasn't sure she would ever get him out of her system.

When she heard Chris and Lem return from town, she scooped up Riley. She met Chris on the back porch. He'd parked her car in the yard.

"Where do you want me to put it?" He held her key in a tight fist.

She shrugged. "Right there is okay I guess."

"Outside?" He cast the sporty car a longing glance over his shoulder.

"For now." She'd ask Griff if there was any room in one of the outbuildings. "Thanks so much. Does it drive okay?"

"Oh, yeah," he said with a sigh.

Jolie smiled to herself and held out her hand for the key. He passed it to her reluctantly.

"If you want me to move it for you, just holler."

"Thanks, Chris."

She forgot about the car and turned back into the house to make lunch. She felt an unwelcome tingle of excitement. Griff would be there shortly.

Griff came out of the barn and stopped and stared at the low-slung silver car gleaming in the noon sun. Did Jolie have a visitor? He immediately thought of the man he suspected she had run from. Had he found her? Was he here to try to force her to go back with him?

He hadn't considered that she might be in danger, but the thought occurred to him now, and a cold ball formed in his gut.

He broke into a jog and hit the back steps at a run. Skidding to a halt on the porch just inside the back door, he saw her head come up and the startled look on her face.

She wiped her hands on a towel and yanked open the door. "What's the matter?"

"Whose car is that?" She was alone in the kitchen.

She glanced past him. "Mine. Why?"

To cover his relief, he turned and looked back at the automobile. This classy woman drove a seriously classy car. "It's done already?"

She'd said she would stay until her car was repaired. The thought of her leaving hit him like a punch to his midsection, surprising him.

"They finished it faster than I expected. Are you ready to eat?"

"Yeah. I'll get cleaned up." He had grease all over his shirt after spending the morning doing some maintenance on the trailer for the old tractor.

"There are clean clothes in the dryer."

He opened the dryer door and pulled the tangle of jeans and shirts into the basket on the floor. The entire load was laced with one-hundred-dollar bills.

"What the—" He pulled on a clean shirt and gathered up the money, then headed into the kitchen.

"Jolie?" He held out the bills.

She looked at the money in his fist and then up at him. "Is it payday?"

He held ten times what he had agreed to pay her. "Not hardly, sweetheart. I found this in the dryer."

She gave him a blank look, then laughed. "I must have forgotten to take it out of my jeans before I put them in the wash."

She took the money from his hand and opened the broom closet, and stuffed it in her purse.

She went back to the counter and finished up the sandwiches. He shook his head as he watched her. Her car, the money, the casual way she accepted both reminded him of the huge gulf between their lifestyles.

He looked around his kitchen. Clean but worn. Old appliances and countertops that had been put in before he was born. The original hardwood floor, complete with the deep gouge in the corner where, as the old story went, his great-grandmother had thrown a hatchet at his great-grandfather during a heated argument.

Jolie looked like an orchid in a weed patch. Cool and elegant and definitely out of place.

Why did she stay?

And what was he going to do when she left?

Chapter Eight

Jolie was upstairs cleaning the bathroom when she heard the pounding on the front door. She pulled off her rubber gloves, stopped long enough to peek at Riley still asleep in his crib and then hurried down the front stairs.

When she pulled open the door, she felt her stomach quake.

There stood her father, Richard Haywood Carleton. He didn't look very happy.

"Hello, Daddy."

"Jolie."

When he scowled at her, Jolie always felt eight years old and in trouble.

She looked past him to a limousine in the front yard. The engine was running.

He looked her up and down, and his disapproval deepened. "Jolie, get your things," he said curtly.

"Daddy, come in." Her stomach quivered. She hated it when her father was unhappy with her.

What a picture she must make, in her jeans and T-shirt, clutching a pair of yellow rubber gloves.

He flapped his hand at her. "Just get your things, Jolie. I'll give you five minutes."

She stalled, trying to work up some courage. "How did you know I was here?" Surely Aunt Rosie hadn't told him.

"I hired a private investigator."

How typical of him, she thought, and her anger sparked. "Dad, come in. I need to close the door."

Reluctantly he stepped into the living room. She gestured to the couch.

He set his jaw and remained standing by the front door. "This defiance has gone on long enough. My plane is at the airport, and we're cleared back to Seattle as soon as we get aboard."

Is that what he thought she was doing? Defying him?

She straightened her shoulders. Be brave, Jolie, be brave. "Dad, you should have called and saved yourself the trip. I'm not leaving. I've made a commitment here."

He looked at her as if she'd grown a second head right in front of his eyes. He opened his mouth to speak, but she cut him off, plunging ahead while she had the courage.

"And then I'm going to go on to Aunt Rosie's for a visit."

Jolie watched her father's face turn red. "Exactly what kind of commitment did you make?"

"I'm taking care of a baby. I'm the nanny."

He gestured to the gloves she clutched in her hand. "And the maid?" He spat out the words as if they left a bad taste in his mouth.

"Yes." She put her hands behind her back so he wouldn't see them shake.

"I didn't raise you to be someone's housekeeper!"
He shouted at her.

Jolie held her ground and took a deep breath. When
he raised his voice, she always ended up in tears and
gave in. Not today, she vowed. Today I live with courage.

Jolie cleared her throat. "Actually, Dad, that's exactly
what you raised me to be."

He stared at her as if she had lost her mind, and he
opened and closed his mouth twice without uttering any
words.

She'd never stood up to him before, and he didn't
seem to know what to do.

She took a bit of reassurance from his loss for words.
"I suppose you thought I would have maids and nannies
to do the work for me, but all you really ever expected
from me was to get married and be someone's wife and
housekeeper."

"That's different!"

"Not really. This is just a little more honest. I'm doing the work myself. Making my own way."

And proud of herself for holding her own in the face
of his anger, but she doubted her father would want to
hear that little bit of news.

His expression changed and his voice softened. "I
need you to come home. I miss you."

She felt her defenses weaken, then realized he was
changing tactics. Intimidation wasn't working so he was
taking another route to get to her. She smiled.

"Dad, between your schedule and mine we sometimes
went a week without having a ten-minute conversation.
You'll be okay until I come home."

He suddenly seemed uncharacteristically hesitant. "I

haven't told you the most important reason you need to come back.''

His new demeanor worried her. She studied him as he paused. He did look a little thinner to her. Was he having health problems?

"Charles has listened to reason. He wants to get married.''

"Charles?'' With a jolt she realized she had given her former fiancé no thought for the past two weeks. "Charles who left me standing in the back of the church? That Charles?''

The scowl was back. "Don't be smart with me, Jolie.''

He spoke to her as if she were a rude child.

She wondered what her father had used to bribe Charles. The thought was so embarrassing. "If Charles has changed his mind, why are you here instead of him?''

He actually sputtered. "Because I'm your father!''

"Dad, I'm not a little girl. I'm not going to come home because you yell at me, or because Charles changed his mind. And when I do come home, I'm not going to marry Charles.''

"Why not?''

"Because he was your choice, not mine. I let myself get pulled along because I didn't want to disappoint you. But I've discovered something in the past few weeks. I need to not disappoint myself.''

"You're acting like an irresponsible teenager.'' He was back to being stiff and angry.

And it's about time she went through some good healthy teenage rebellion, Jolie thought. She'd needed to grow up.

Impatiently her father pulled back the sleeve of his

suit coat and glanced at his watch. "I have to go. I'm due in New York for a meeting tomorrow."

"I thought you said you were going back to Seattle."

"If you refuse to be reasonable, I might as well go directly to my meeting."

Jolie suspected if she'd agreed to go with him, she would have ended up in New York. Her father didn't mind inconvenience as long as it wasn't his own.

"I hope it all goes well. I'll call you when I leave for Aunt Rosie's."

His face tight with anger, he turned and left without saying goodbye. She watched him get in the limousine. He never glanced back.

She closed the door. Trembling, she leaned against it.

Her father always got what he wanted. In business and with her. He would consider this afternoon to be in the loss column because he didn't get what he came for.

She sighed and wondered how long he'd remain angry. She'd always buckled under to him because she was so scared he would...

What?

Stop loving her?

She felt shaky and plopped down on the couch, dropping her spinning head between her knees.

What a light-bulb moment.

All her life she'd obeyed him instantly out of fear. But she knew he loved her. Her thoughts were so jumbled that she didn't hear Griff enter the room.

She jumped when he knelt in front of her and put both his hands on her shoulders. He pushed her upright and studied her face.

His angry expression made her jerk back against the couch.

He searched her features. "Did the bastard hurt you?"

"No!" Her father would never hurt her.

"Was he the man you're running from?" He gentled his hold on her and ran his big hands up and down her arms in a soothing way, distracting her.

What was he talking about? "I'm not running from anyone." She'd preferred to think she was running toward something, but just now she wasn't sure.

He gave her a skeptical look. "Who the hell was he?"

"My father. He just stopped by to say hello."

And wonder of wonders, she'd stood up to him.

Griff let go of her and stood up, then turned and sat beside her on the couch, pulling her into his arms.

"You're shaking. Are you sure you're okay?" he whispered into her hair.

She looked up into his incredible blue eyes and saw the concern there for her. Jolie put her hand on his cheek.

"I'm really fine. He's angry with me, but when he has time to think things over, I'm sure he'll understand."

He stared at her for a minute, then lowered his head until his lips brushed against hers.

Her heart thumped in her chest and she turned into his arms.

"Jolie—"

Whatever he was going to say was cut off by a wail from upstairs.

Riley had learned to let her know when he woke up. Today his timing was lousy.

Griff let her go and stood up abruptly. He shoved his hands deep in his pockets. "I'll get him for you."

She wanted to reach out and grab him and tell him Riley would wait. Instead she watched him take the stairs two at a time. He was trying so hard with Riley. The baby was really starting to respond to him, too.

He came back down with Riley perched on his hip. Griff swung him around until the baby squealed, then handed him to Jolie.

"Time to get back to work." He turned and walked out the back door.

Jolie nuzzled Riley as she watched Griff go, wondering what he had been about to say before they were interrupted.

It seemed to Jolie both the Price men were cursed with bad timing.

Chapter Nine

After lunch Jolie sat down to plan the week's menus. She had the newspaper, full of ads for specials on holiday turkeys, spread all over the kitchen table.

Griff walked in the kitchen and glanced at what she was doing. "I usually spend Thanksgiving with the Morgans."

The Morgans owned the ranch next to the Circle P. Jolie nodded at Griff's comment, not knowing if he was telling her he would be leaving her alone and going by himself, or if she would be included in the holiday celebration.

Thanksgiving. She'd never been away from family for the holiday. Some of the hands would probably be around. She could cook a turkey and have whoever was here join her.

"Jolie?"

She realized he had been saying something to her. "What?"

"I asked if you wanted to go with me."

"Oh, yes I would," she said, relieved and pleased to be included.

"Fine." He studied her for a long moment, his sky-blue eyes giving no hint of what he was thinking, then left through the back door.

She stared after him. He always seemed about to say something, then he'd stop and leave. Not only did his habit of staring at her intently leave her flustered, it sent chills up her spine.

She was far too aware of the man. That alone told her she needed to make plans to leave.

Jolie hadn't intended to be here this long. Her car had been repaired for over a week, and she still had plenty of money to make the drive to Aunt Rosie in New York.

She and Griff hadn't discussed finding a new nanny. She'd pushed away the thought of turning Riley over to a stranger. He was making so much progress with her and with Griff.

And then there was Griff. She tried to tell herself she was staying because of the baby, but the man had become a powerful draw. Too powerful.

She knew she walked a fine line with him.

The longer she stayed, the harder it became to resist him. And resist him she must.

He'd been hurt so badly by his wife and brother. Jolie knew he'd welcome a casual affair with no strings. She'd been hurt too, but it had affected her feelings a different way. When she found the right man, she wouldn't settle for less than a total commitment.

She wanted a family, a solid marriage. Griff wasn't ready for that. He might never be ready again for that.

Sadness for him swamped her. He was too hurt to try again for happiness.

* * *

Griff hollered up the stairs. "Are you almost ready? We're late."

What was she doing up there? She'd said she was almost ready before he'd brought the truck around to the front of the house and transferred the baby seat from her car.

There was no way he was going to try to fold his long legs into the passenger seat of her car and let her drive.

What the heck was taking her so long? He didn't want to miss the kickoff for the game. He rarely took a day off, but he planned to enjoy every minute of this Thanksgiving.

"I'll be there in a minute." Her voice drifted down the stairs.

He rested his elbow on the banister as he waited for her, thinking how nice it would be to spend the day with her. And the baby. He was actually getting used to being around the little guy. Riley's antics amused him.

Somewhere along the way he had stopped seeing the kid as a symbol of Jake and Deirdre's betrayal. He needed to mention that to Jolie and thank her. In fact, he had a lot to thank her for. Unfortunately, he had a hard time finding the right words.

When they were alone, he thought much more about getting her in his bed than he did about talking.

"Okay, we're ready." She appeared at the top of the stairs, dressed in tailored slacks and a soft pink sweater that clung to her curves. She held the baby in her arms and had a huge bag slung over her shoulder.

He recognized the bag. It matched the luggage he'd dragged into the house the day she arrived.

Was she leaving? He felt the bottom drop out of his stomach. He took the stairs two at a time, until he stopped on the step below where she was standing.

Eye-to-eye, she gave him a wary look, but held her ground as he slipped the bag off her shoulder. It weighed a ton.

"What is this?" He held the bag up.

She gave him a puzzled look. "Things for the baby. Diapers, blanket, a change of clothes. Why?"

He felt a surge of relief that he had no intention of investigating closely. "How can one little baby need all this stuff?"

She laughed. "Oh, you'd be surprised."

The warm scent of her perfume made him want to lean in close and nibble on her neck. He shifted his body, and Riley picked that moment to reach out and grab his nose.

Griff laughed, pulled back and carried the bag down the stairs.

He waited while she grabbed her jacket out of the hall closet, and held the front door open for her. He stowed the bag in the back seat of the cab of his truck.

She had one foot on the running board and was trying to hoist the baby up into the high cab. He hooked an arm around her waist and pulled her back down, liking the feel of her up against him.

"I'll do that." He lifted Riley out of her arms and settled him into his seat.

Jolie had scrambled into the front seat and turned around to watch him.

Keeping one hand on the baby to anchor him in the seat he asked, "How does this rig work?" The car seat had a bar and a series of straps and buckles.

"I'll buckle him in. You watch." Jolie leaned over the front seat and brought the straps across the baby's chest, explaining the process.

He watched, all right. As she moved, her sweater

pulled taut against her breasts. Dry-mouthed, Griff stayed where he was for a moment, admiring the view until he felt a definite change in the fit of his jeans. If he didn't get his mind off her he was in for a very uncomfortable drive to the Morgans'.

He closed the back door and walked around the back of the truck, stopping to check a tire to give himself a little more time. He opened the driver's door and slid into the seat with just a minimum of discomfort, congratulating himself on his control.

She certainly was a fine-looking woman. With a little coaxing he just might be able to get her into his bed. She wasn't immune to him. He knew that from the way she reacted when he kissed her. His mouth curved at the thought, and once again his jeans got too tight.

"Griff?"

Her soft voice jerked him away from his pleasant thoughts. "What?"

"How far is it to the Morgans'?"

He glanced over at her. "By the road it's ten miles."

She smiled and looked out the windshield. "And you're next-door neighbors."

What a city girl she was. Her neighbors in Seattle were probably only yards away. She was unsuited to Montana and out of her element. That thought reminded him of the incident with the snake and he swallowed a chuckle. The hands were still laughing over that one in the bunkhouse.

"Does it bother you, being out here?" He hadn't really given much thought to what it must be like for her.

She looked surprised and didn't answer for a moment. "No. I guess I've been so busy I..."

Her voice trailed off, and he got the impression she had decided not to say what she really thought. The city girl was being polite. He reminded himself to not ask that question again because he had a feeling he wouldn't like the answer.

They pulled up in front of the Morgans' and he parked next to another truck he recognized. He hadn't seen Vince Morgan since last Thanksgiving, and he missed his best friend from high school. Vince must have driven down from Boise.

Griff got the baby out and handed him to Jolie, then grabbed the bag from the floor and led her up the wide steps of the Morgans' house. This home had been built at about the same time as his, but in a completely different style. Made out of stone and logs, it sprawled on the top of a knoll and had a 360-degree view of Morgan land.

Griff had spent a lot of time here after his mother left. Vince's mom, Kathy, had folded him into her large family and treated him like one of her own. It had made his teenage years a little easier. He'd never told her how much it had meant to him.

Vince opened the door and pulled him into a bear hug, thumping him on the back.

"Griff, good to see you." He let go of Griff and turned to Jolie, letting his eyes run down her form. "Welcome. Come in."

Griff didn't like the way his friend was smiling at Jolie. He'd seen Vince turn on the charm before and knew women had a hard time resisting him.

"Vince, this is Jolie Carleton, Riley's nanny." He helped Jolie out of her jacket.

Vince raised an eyebrow and nodded, a big smile spreading over his face. "Pleased to meet you."

Griff felt the need to pull Vince's attention away from Jolie. "When did you get in?"

"Late last night."

"Did you bring Sally?" Griff remembered his girl-friend from last year.

"Old news. She took a job on the East Coast." He gave Jolie another look.

She smiled up at Vince. "Thank you for inviting me."

Vince returned her smile, then turned to Griff and, in a low voice, said, "I heard about Jake. I'm sorry for your loss."

Griff nodded to his oldest friend, noting that Vince didn't include Deirdre. Vince had never liked her.

Griff was a little surprised that the hurt he usually felt at people's condolences had faded.

Griff broke the awkward silence. "Where's your mom?"

Vince laughed. "Where else? The kitchen."

Griff introduced Jolie to everyone they encountered on the way to the kitchen and didn't miss her over-whelmed expression.

"Don't worry. There isn't going to be a test."

"I just didn't expect there would be so many people. I feel as if I'm intruding."

"Intruding? No one is better at welcoming folks than the Morgans." They walked past the long dining room table, set with gleaming china and silver.

She nodded, looking a little more reassured. "If you say so."

Griff pushed open the kitchen door and they were im-mediately enveloped by the fragrant warmth. "Kathy. Happy Thanksgiving."

Kathy Morgan turned from the stove, and her round, freckled face lit up at the sight of him. She hurried across the kitchen, wiping her hands on her big white apron.

"Griff! Happy Thanksgiving!" Her gaze strayed to Jolie as she pulled him into a hug.

When she let him go, he turned and motioned to Jolie. "Kathy, this is Jolie Carleton, Riley's nanny."

"Welcome, Jolie. I'm glad you could come."

She eyed the baby, then looked up at Griff. "I don't suppose this little guy would let me hold him?"

Jolie nuzzled Riley's hair and smiled. "You can try. I don't know how he is with strangers."

As Kathy reached for the baby, Griff was struck by Jolie's comment. Kathy was one of his favorite people and to Riley, she was a stranger.

As soon as Kathy had the baby in her arms, he stiffened up and his lower lip began to quiver.

Kathy gave him a quick kiss and handed the baby back. "Too much too soon."

Riley grabbed Jolie's sweater and hung on as if he were afraid of being dropped.

Kathy ran her hand over the baby's curls and smiled at him. "We have time, don't we, Riley?"

Jolie shifted the baby onto her hip and asked, "What can I do to help?"

Kathy shook her head and shooed them out of the kitchen. "At this point it's a one-woman show. Griff, you get Jolie something to drink and go watch the game."

Jolie started to protest, and Griff slid his palm to the small of her back to nudge her along.

When the door had swung closed behind them, he said, "Kathy will ask when she wants help."

"There are so many people to feed and—"

"And Kathy loves it that way. It's like this every Thanksgiving and Christmas."

Griff introduced her to Vince's two sisters, Shauna and Jenny, who also balanced babies on their hips.

The women smiled at her and introduced their toddlers, a boy and a girl who looked to be a few months older than Riley.

Griff felt uncomfortable, surrounded by women and babies. "Do you want anything to drink?"

She smiled. "No, I'm fine."

A cheer of all-male voices rolled out of the den, and he looked longingly in that direction. "Want to watch the game?"

She looked at the other women, who both shook their heads, then back at Griff. "Not really. Go ahead."

"Okay." Relieved, he nodded to the women, then headed for the den.

Jolie watched him go, then turned back to Vince's sisters.

Shauna spoke first, her voice lowered. "How's he doing?"

Jolie was reluctant to answer, then realized they'd known Griff all their lives. This wasn't gossip, this was genuine concern for a friend.

"I'm not sure. He doesn't say much." And it was all he didn't say that concerned her the most.

Shauna shifted the toddler she carried and scowled. "I knew the minute I met Deirdre she was going to be trouble. I just didn't realize how much."

Jenny smiled sadly and teased her sister. "You had such a crush on Griff you wouldn't have liked any woman he brought home."

Shauna blushed. "That may be true, but you can't tell me you liked her."

Jenny shrugged. "At first. She was so sophisticated.

The clothes, the makeup. All that style. Too much to be happy here.''

"Too bad when she decided to run off she stole what meant the most to Griff.''

Jolie couldn't help herself. She had to ask. "What was that?''

"Griff's brother, Jake. They were so close. I think losing Jake was much harder than losing Deirdre.''

"Yeah, first his daddy, then Jake. It was a hard year.''

Jolie recalled the photo of the two boys and the man she had found facedown in the dresser. "But if she didn't like the life here, why would she run off with Griff's brother?''

"You had to know Jake. The man was, well, exciting. He was as good-looking as Griff, but he had this easy charm that just sucked a woman in.''

"Yup. If pheromones are what attract a woman to a man, Jake had more than his share. And he was a rodeo star. I'm sure his life looked a whole lot more exciting than being a rancher's wife.''

"Wild Man.'' Jolie murmured, remembering Jake's nickname.

"Yeah. He'd had that name since he was just a little guy.'' She gestured toward a corner of the living room. "Let's go and sit down. Cloe weighs a ton.''

The little girl wiggled out of her mother's arms as soon as they were seated and made a beeline for a basket of toys beside the couch.

Her cousin, Matthew, trailed in her wake. Riley still had a death grip on Jolie's sweater. She held him close to reassure him. She'd let him go at his own speed.

He watched the other children with an avid interest as the women chatted about children, the price of beef and the weather.

Jolie liked these two women. They seemed to enjoy their lives and adore their roles as wives and mothers. Too many of the women she knew left the raising of their children to others.

With a shock, she realized that until recently she'd probably had more in common with Griff's wife than she had with Shauna and Jenny.

"Shauna, watch Cloe for a minute while I check and see if Mama needs any help."

"Sure. Ask her how long it's going to be. I'm starving."

The smells of turkey and stuffing were making Jolie's mouth water. Riley would want to eat soon, too.

Riley pushed away from her and wiggled off her lap, standing clinging to her knee. He was still avidly watching the two toddlers play.

"Is he walking yet?"

"No. He's still crawling. But he has started to pull himself up and stand." Jolie felt protective of Riley and wasn't going to discuss her worries about his development.

Besides, she thought, as she rubbed Riley's back with an absent gesture, he had made great strides in the past two weeks.

Jenny returned and announced that dinner was almost ready. They scooped up the babies and made their way to the dining room, where the sisters pulled high chairs out of the corners and settled their children.

"We don't have another chair. Will he be okay on your lap?

"Sure." And on her lap was where she wanted him. Jolie loved the weight of him leaning against her.

She chose a chair near the door in case she had to leave the table. The men wandered in from the den and she found herself seated between Vince and Jenny's husband. Griff chose a seat across and down the table from her. Assorted aunts, uncles and cousins filled in all the available spaces.

The men argued over the calls made by the referees for the game they'd just watched and discussed the possible outcome of the game they all intended to watch after the meal.

Shauna, Jenny and Kathy carried in bowls and platters heaped with turkey, stuffing, potatoes and vegetables. Kathy, still in her apron, settled at the foot of the table and signaled her husband to start the blessing. His big voice rang out as they bowed their heads, and the prayer of Thanksgiving was ended with a hearty group Amen.

Plates and friendly insults were passed around the table. Jolie felt the love and friendship contained in the room. Even though these people were strangers, they were welcoming and warm and real.

Right in the middle of serving herself green beans, she realized that this was the best Thanksgiving she had ever had. She was in the middle of a roomful of strangers and she was having the time of her life.

Lost in thought, Jolie looked down and found Riley's hands in her food. "Oh, no!"

"Here, let me help." Vince piled food on her plate while she wiped the baby's hands.

"Thanks. That's more than enough."

"You haven't tasted Mom's cooking. Everyone comes back for seconds."

She smiled at him, fairly sure she wouldn't be able to finish what was on her plate, then concentrated on getting some food into Riley.

When the baby was finally full, she shifted him to her shoulder and tried to eat with one hand.

Vince leaned over and plucked Riley off her shoulder. "Let me have him while you finish eating. Do you want another plate? That food is probably cold."

To Jolie's surprise, Riley didn't seem to mind Vince holding him. She put her hand on Vince's sleeve to keep him in his chair. "No, really, this is fine."

She felt guilty letting him hold the baby when he probably wanted to fill his plate again.

She was cutting her turkey when she felt someone looking at her. She looked up.

Griff scowled at her.

Immediately she felt guilty. She should be taking care of the baby, not imposing on Vince. Appetite gone, she scraped back her chair and reached for Riley.

Vince looked startled at her sudden move.

She groped for an excuse. "I, ah, need to change him."

Jolie left the dining room and grabbed a diaper and changing pad out of the bag in the living room. Just as she was laying Riley down, Griff appeared in the doorway.

"What's the matter?"

She looked up at him as she knelt by the couch. To her relief he no longer looked angry. "Nothing."

"Why did you leave the table in such a hurry?"

"I needed to change the baby." And, she wanted to add, when you scowl at me like that you make me nervous.

She stripped off Riley's wet diaper and slid a new one under him. Griff was still standing by the door.

She fastened the tabs and looked up at him again. If he was going to scold her, why didn't he just do it and get it over with? "Why are you standing there staring at me?"

"I wanted to warn you about Vince."

That was the last thing Jolie had expected him to say. "Warn me about what?"

"Women fall for him all the time."

Jolie opened her mouth to say something, then closed it with a snap. She had no retort.

"I thought you should know." He looked as if he was going to say something else, then he stopped.

She hated when he did that.

"Thank you for the warning." She turned back to Riley, concentrating on matching up the snaps on his overalls. What had that been about?

He nodded and walked away. She watched him disappear, and then the thought struck her. He was jealous. Of Vince. A warm little glow started in her midsection.

Griff was jealous. That meant he had feelings for her. She leaned over and kissed Riley soundly, feeling better than she had in days.

Her hands stilled. Is that what she wanted? For Griff to have feelings about her?

It would be so easy to have a fling with him before she left, so easy to give in to what he had made very clear he wanted.

Easy. And very stupid.

She finished snapping up Riley's overalls and glanced at his face to see why he was being so quiet. The child was fast asleep. Poor little guy, all the excitement had worn him out.

She was contemplating what she should do with him when Shauna came into the living room.

"Everything okay?"

Jolie nodded at Riley. "He's not used to so much excitement."

Shauna pulled an afghan off the couch and spread it

on the floor. "They're dropping like flies. Mattie fell asleep in his mashed potatoes. I'll put him in here, too, so we can keep an eye on them."

Jolie transferred Riley from the couch to the floor. She returned to the table and settled in her chair, feeling Griff's eyes on her. "Where's the baby?"

Conversation at the table stopped and Jolie felt as if everyone was watching them.

"He fell asleep." She gestured at Shauna, who was trying to wipe the mashed potatoes out of Mattie's hair without waking him. "The boys are going to nap in the living room."

Griff nodded and went back to eating, but he kept watching her as she finished her dinner and talked to Vince.

Vince wasn't flirting with her, and it still seemed to bother Griff.

Jolie helped the other women with the dishes and took turns checking on the babies. Kathy and her daughters had a warm relationship that Jolie envied. She'd been very young when her own mother died, and she'd not become close with either of her stepmothers, feeling like an unwanted accessory that had come with the marriages.

Vince wandered into the kitchen and picked up a towel to help with the drying. From the look his sisters exchanged, this was not something he did very often.

He maneuvered himself until he was standing beside her. "You enjoying your stay in Montana?"

She smiled up at him, trying to find the right words. "It's beautiful. So open and, well, big."

"Yeah, big." He grinned back.

"Where do you live?" She knew he had driven in from somewhere.

"Boise. I took over a spread owned by my uncle about five years ago."

The kitchen door swung open and Griff stood there holding Riley. The baby was rubbing at his eyes and yawning.

"Time to go." His tone was abrupt.

"Okay." She handed the towel to Vince and reached to take the baby. Riley held out his arms, and she scooped him against her.

Griff walked over to Kathy and kissed her on the cheek. "Thanks for having us. It was great, as always."

Jolie echoed her thank-you.

Kathy, giving Jolie a long look, said, "Don't be a stranger."

Jolie smiled and murmured a noncommittal comment. She didn't want to start a discussion about how long she would be staying.

They said goodbye to everyone on their way out, and Griff silently loaded the baby into his car seat.

When they were finally all settled in the cab and on their way, Jolie turned to Griff. "Is something wrong?"

"No." He kept his eyes straight ahead.

After more silence and several more miles had passed, Jolie said, "Thank you for inviting me."

Griff looked over at her. "Probably not what you're used to for a holiday."

"No, it wasn't." Usually she and her father went to the country club and had dinner with each other, or a stepmother if there happened to be one in the picture at the time. Then they would return home. That would be the extent of the holiday. A turkey dinner fixed by someone else. No family, no lively discussions during the meal, no children to watch.

Jolie wondered what it would be like to really belong

here, to be a part of Griff's life. She sneaked a peek at his beautiful profile. What would it be like to pack up their children and spend the day with the Morgan family, then drive home and put sleepy children to bed and spend some time together, just the two of them?

Suddenly she realized that was exactly what she wanted. Not a brief affair. She wanted a whole life. With him.

To head up the stairs at the end of the day and look in on their offspring before they went to bed. To wake up in his arms in the morning and wait for him to come home at night.

"Jolie?"

She realized they were home. "What?"

"Are you okay?" He eyed her closely.

"I'm fine." She managed a smile as she turned to unbuckle Riley's car seat belt.

But she wasn't fine. She felt like a raw nerve. She'd been attracted to him from the minute he'd walked into the diner.

When had she fallen in love with Griff? It had sneaked up on her.

"Are you sure you're okay?"

No, she wanted to shout, I'm not fine. I love you, and you act like you don't even like me half the time.

There was no way she was going to tell him how she felt and open herself up to that kind of hurt.

"I'm fine, really." Actually she was going to cry.

He was still staring at her as he pulled Riley from his seat and handed him over. "I have to go down to the barn."

"Good, that's good. You go ahead." She hurried up the front steps and into the house.

When she looked back through the window in the front door he was standing by the truck, watching her.

Well, he didn't have to ever find out how she felt. He didn't have the same feelings, and getting dumped once in a month was about her limit.

She carried the baby up the stairs and let the tears fall when she was sure he couldn't see her anymore.

Chapter Ten

Griff watched Jolie race up the steps to the house as if her tail was on fire. What the heck had happened in the truck on the way home?

She'd had the look of a woman who was going to cry.

He headed for the barn and tried to remember what little conversation they'd had.

Maybe Vince had said something to upset her. But she'd seemed fine when they left the Morgans.

Griff rubbed his hand over the back of his neck. If he lived to be one hundred he probably would never understand women.

He checked in with the hands, then went to inspect the generator. The weather was turning cold, and they'd need it before long.

His thoughts drifted back to Jolie. She really seemed to enjoy the gathering at the Morgans. She probably was used to parties and going out to dinner.

She hadn't taken a day off since she got here. Caring

for a baby was like running a ranch. Twenty-four-hour-a-day operation.

He'd tell her to go out Saturday night. Riley went to bed around seven. He'd tell her about some of the nicer bars in Billings. On the weekends they had live music and dancing.

Then he pictured her being hit on by a bunch of guys and felt a twist in his gut. He didn't like the image at all.

He could use an evening out himself. One of the hands could come over and stay at the house after the baby went to bed. He'd escort her to town. That way he could keep an eye on her and be there if any of the single guys got too friendly.

That sounded like a much better plan. He checked the fuel supply for the generator and headed back to the house.

Jolie was in the kitchen with her head in the refrigerator when he came through the back door. She had changed into jeans and a sweatshirt.

She looked up and smiled. She'd recovered from whatever had been bothering her, he noted with relief.

"Where's the baby?"

"I put him to bed. He was exhausted from his big day. Are you hungry for supper?"

"I could eat."

She turned back to the refrigerator and pulled out makings for sandwiches. He watched her graceful movements.

"Listen, I was thinking. You haven't had a day off since you got here."

She shrugged and continued to make sandwiches.

"You could go into Billings on Saturday night."

She hesitated, then turned to look at him. "Thanks,

but I wouldn't feel comfortable out at night by myself. I don't know Billings that well and—''

''I'd drive you in.''

''Who'd stay with Riley?''

''We could leave after he goes to sleep. Chris or Lem could come over and watch TV.''

''Are you thinking of going to a movie?''

''If you want. But there's this great bar you might like with live music, dancing and good burgers.''

She hesitated again. ''I guess so.''

She was starting to annoy him. Usually when he asked a woman out she was glad to say yes. ''You need to think about it for a while?''

''No. I was just thinking if Riley were to wake up and...''

''He knows Chris and Lem. He'll be fine.''

''It's not a good idea to let a child wake up and find himself with strangers...''

Annoyed, he cocked an eyebrow at her. She sure was full of excuses. ''Says who? And they're not strangers.''

''All right. What time?''

She made it sound as if he was offering her a ride to the dentist for a root canal.

''Seven should be fine.'' That would get them into town in enough time to eat dinner and get in some dancing. Neither of them needed a late night. He had his cows and she had to get up with the baby.

She looked as if she was going to say more, then she put his sandwich in front of him and sat down. He shouldn't be hungry since the huge meal he'd consumed at the Morgans, but the sandwich tasted great.

Jolie picked her way through half her meal, then started to excuse herself.

Something was really bothering her. Griff reached out

and put his hand on her forearm to stop her from getting up. "What's the matter?"

"Nothing. I'm just not very hungry after that huge meal at the Morgans'."

"Did Vince say something to upset you?"

She stared at him for a moment, then gave a little hoot of laughter that had an edge to it. "No."

She shook him off and left him sitting and wondering at the odd expression on her face when he had asked about Vince. Like he had told himself earlier, he was never going to understand women.

Jolie spent the week keeping her distance from Griff, trying to talk herself out of being in love. If you could fall in, you could fall out, she reasoned, especially this early, before anything happened.

He had only asked her out because he was taking pity on her for being cooped up. She'd been feeling housebound and an evening out would feel good.

She didn't have to let him know how she felt about him. In fact, it would be a perfect opportunity to bring up the subject of finding a permanent nanny for Riley.

On Saturday afternoon Jolie put Riley down for his nap and then called Vince's sister Shauna.

"What do I wear to go into Billings and go dancing?"

"That's easy. Jeans. Everybody wears jeans."

"Out at night?"

"You bet. You wear anything else and you'll stick out like a sore thumb. Who are you going out with?"

"Griff's giving me a ride to town."

There was silence, then Shauna said, "Ah."

Annoyed, Jolie shot back, "There's no 'ah.' It's just a night out."

"Sure it is. You have a good time." Shauna laughed and hung up.

Jolie headed for her closet. She didn't know about wearing jeans, but she didn't want to stick out, either.

She settled on a pair of designer jeans she had brought with her from Seattle and a white silk blouse.

She took a shower and washed her hair while the baby was still asleep. He was so mobile now that she couldn't manage to get that done while he was awake.

She fixed his dinner and fed him, then brought him upstairs to her room while she dressed.

As she stepped into her silk panties and matching bra she heard Griff come in, and the clunk of the water pipes let her know he was showering too.

She felt all shivery with anticipation. When was the last time she had felt this way? She couldn't remember, and that made her sad. She had to keep reminding herself Griff didn't have feelings for her.

She gave herself a little shake as she buttoned her shirt and pulled on her jeans. Tonight was for fun, nothing more, nothing less. And to talk about hiring her replacement.

She glanced around the room and realized she had lost track of Riley. She found him sitting on the floor of her closet, chewing on a shoe.

"Yuck!" She scooped him up and threw the shoe back in the closet. "We can find you something better than that to chew on."

She heard Griff's footsteps go past her door. She carried Riley to his room and dressed him for bed, then took him downstairs to fix him a bottle.

Chris knocked at the back door, and she called for him to come in.

He stood in the door to the kitchen and gave a low

whistle as he took off his hat. "You look mighty nice tonight, Miss Jolie."

She loved the quaint politeness all Griff's hands showed her.

"Thank you, Chris. Are you sure you're okay with this? I'm sure he'll go right to bed, but…"

"Don't you waste any time worrying over me and the boy, here. We'll get along just fine."

But Jolie was worried. She had never left Riley with anyone else and there was so much he needed to know.

"The doctor's number is on the refrigerator. You have to watch him all the time because he crawls now. And he puts everything in his mouth. And he likes to explore things like the electrical outlets. And if he wakes up after you put him to bed you need to check his diaper and—"

"Jolie, darlin', take a breath."

She turned to see Griff standing in the door and forgot what else she was going to say. He'd shaved and put on a blue shirt that made his eyes even more beautiful. New-looking jeans hugged his lean hips, and fancy boots added to his already considerable height. He looked… delicious.

Jolie remembered to breathe. "I was just giving Chris instructions."

"We're going to be gone for a few hours, not years."

She felt herself blushing. "I know, but Chris doesn't have any experience."

Chris let out a whoop of laughter. "I'm the oldest of ten kids. Riley and I will do fine."

Griff nodded to Chris. "I'll leave my phone on. Call if you have a problem."

Jolie gave Riley a kiss and handed him off to Chris. She waited for a reaction. The baby looked at Chris and then back at her, his lip quivering. Chris reached into a back pocket and produced a carved wooden animal, let the baby see it, then dropped it in his shirt pocket.

Attention diverted, Riley was absorbed with the effort of trying to remove the toy from Chris's shirt pocket.

Griff dropped her jacket over her shoulders and took her by the arm. "Come on, let's go."

"But—"

"Jolie." His voice held a gentle warning.

She sighed and turned to go. He was right. She had to start getting Riley used to the idea of being left with someone else. She just hadn't expected it to be so hard.

As they walked out the front door, Riley decided that Jolie leaving wasn't such a good idea and began to wail. She tried to turn and go back to him, but Griff pulled her onto the porch and closed the door firmly behind him.

She could still hear the baby's cries. Griff kept his hand on her arm and drew her down the steps.

"Keep moving. He'll be fine."

"I know, but…"

He helped her up into the truck. She wanted so badly to bolt back into the house and reassure Riley, but she knew that would only make things worse, so she sat miserably quiet and they drove away from the house.

When they got to the main road, Griff stopped the truck and handed her his phone.

She looked up at him in surprise.

"Go ahead and call Chris. You're going to be miserable if you don't."

She quickly punched in the number and waited as the phone in the kitchen rang. Chris picked it up on the third ring.

"Price Ranch."

She didn't hear any crying in the background. "Chris, it's Jolie. Is Riley okay?"

"Sure is. He stopped crying before your taillights disappeared. Stop worrying and have fun."

"Thanks." She blew out a breath of relief and disconnected the call.

"Feel better?" Griff smiled at her.

"Yes. Thanks."

They drove into Billings in companionable silence and parked in front of a shingled building with a neon sign announcing the name Rounders.

Griff came around and helped her from the truck. She enjoyed the courtesy. It made her feel special.

He opened the door for her and she was hit by a wall of noise and music, the smell of grilled meat and beer. Bodies crowded on and around a large dance floor in the huge room.

Neon signs cast colored lights over the people standing at the bar and an old-fashioned mirrored disco ball tagged the dancers with moving squares of light. Griff put his hand on the small of her back and guided her around the dance floor toward an empty table along the far wall.

He helped her out of her jacket. "Things are really hopping tonight, and it's still early."

Jolie was dazzled by the noise and lights and music. Everyone seemed to be having fun and laughing. Usually the social gatherings she attended were much more sedate and quiet.

"You okay?" Griff asked, looking down at her.

"Oh, yes. It's wonderful, all the energy. I like this place."

He grinned at her as he pulled out her chair. "Just wait until things start to heat up."

She settled into the big wooden chair and tried to imagine things getting more lively than they were right now.

Griff took the seat across from her. "Hungry?"

She had skipped lunch while she tried to figure out what to wear. "I'm starving!"

He handed her a slightly sticky menu from the stack propped between the ketchup and mustard bottles on the end of the table.

"Aren't you going to eat?" she asked when he didn't take a menu for himself.

"I know what I want. They make the best burgers here you've ever tasted."

She handed the menu back to him without looking at it. "Then that's what I'll have."

A cute little brunette waitress arrived and greeted Griff by name. "You haven't been in for a while, sugar." She looked over at Jolie and smiled.

"Hey, Marla. How are you?"

"Fine, just fine. What can I get you?"

"We'll both have the house special, and I'd like a beer." He looked at Jolie. "What would you like to drink?"

She had seen nothing but beer mugs on the tables as they came in. Not a wineglass in sight. "I'll have a beer, too."

"Okay. Two burgers and two beers. Be up right quick." Marla bestowed another smile on Griff and turned away.

Jolie watched Marla leave and wondered if she and Griff had dated, or if Marla would like to. She had definitely sensed some female interest on Marla's part, and felt a little sting of jealousy.

"Come on, we have time for a dance before the food arrives."

He pulled out her chair and folded her hand into his big, warm one. She could feel the calluses against her skin. It felt like an honest hand, the hand of a man who made his living by really working.

He pulled her toward the dance floor, and she realized that people were doing some kind of synchronized dance.

Jolie stopped and tugged on Griff's hand. "I don't know how to dance like that."

"Don't worry. It's easy to catch on. We'll stand behind everyone and I'll show you." He pulled on her hand and towed her to the back of the dance floor.

She eyed the dancers and thought he might be a little optimistic. It looked complicated to her.

The music was louder out on the floor and he had to lean down to talk to her. She liked the feel of his breath on her face. In fact, she thought with a sigh, she liked everything about him.

"Every dance is just a series of repetitions of a few basic steps." He stood on her left, still holding her hand and did a series of steps to the right and the left.

Jolie tried to follow him, but got tangled up. Griff moved behind Jolie and put his hands on her waist and leaned down to murmur the directions in her ear. The feel of his big warm body behind her and the weight of his hands on her waist made her feel as if she were melting.

She struggled to pay attention to his directions as she watched the people in front of her. By the time the music ended, she was catching on.

Marla skirted the dance floor with a huge tray on her shoulder and signaled to Griff. They returned to the table. Marla had put down two platters heaped with food and two giant mugs of beer.

Jolie eyed the meal in dismay. A huge hamburger smothered in cheese and grilled onions sat in the middle of the plate surrounded by french fries, onion rings and a large mound of coleslaw. It looked like more than she could eat in a week.

She glanced up and caught Griff grinning at her. "Bit off more than you can chew?"

"You forgot to mention the size of the house special." She cut the burger in half and still had to hold it with both hands.

She took a sip of her beer and liked the yeasty taste of it. She made it through half the burger before she had to stop or risk maximum discomfort. Griff had polished off his meal so she offered him the other half of hers. He finished that off, too.

"I think maybe I'm still not feeding you enough." To her surprise he looked a little sheepish. "What?"

"Well, sometimes after we eat I go down and have a bowl of chili at the cookshack."

She thought of the large meals he consumed in the kitchen. "Why didn't you say something?"

He squirmed a little in his seat. "That first night when you fixed the salad you looked like you were going to cry when I asked for more."

She smiled at him. "I did not!"

He shrugged. She realized he used that response when he didn't want to talk about something. She tucked that little tidbit away.

"Come on, let's dance." He came around and held her chair.

On the way to the back of the dance floor he greeted

several people he knew but didn't stop to talk. Jolie was aware of the assessing glances coming her way.

He coached her as he had before, and by the third number she caught on. She liked the feel of his hands at her waist and on her shoulder as he took her through the steps. The music and the noise and friendly people around her blended together into a pleasant, warm atmosphere.

There were more and more things she was going to miss about Montana when she left.

Griff cupped her chin and tilted her face up. "What's the matter, darlin'?"

She managed a smile for him. She wanted to have the courage to tell him she loved him. Instead she said, "Nothing. I guess I'm getting a little tired."

He glanced at the clock over the bar surrounded by neon announcing Miller Time. "Well, it is after ten."

"So late?" The evening had flown by, and she'd barely thought of Riley. And she hadn't brought up the subject of a new nanny.

Jolie stifled a yawn. Days on the ranch started early, and she hadn't been up this late since she had arrived.

"Ready to go?"

"I suppose we should." She felt a little like Cinderella approaching midnight.

They went back to the table and he paid the bill, grabbed their jackets and headed for the door. As they stepped out into the frigid evening, the contrast to the hot noisy bar was extreme.

Stars glittered with a cold bright light that took her breath away. A full moon coated the buildings in a silvery glow.

"Oh," she breathed, "what a beautiful night." She turned to thank him for the fun evening.

His arm came around her waist and before she could think, he had his mouth on hers and she was sinking into the kiss.

He stepped back, leaving her dazed. "I've been wanting to do that all evening."

He opened the door to the truck for her, and all her befuddled mind could come up with was, Well why didn't you?

"Are you going to get in?" He grinned at her.

"Oh, of course." Head spinning, she stepped up onto the seat and he closed the door.

They drove back in silence, Jolie lost in thoughts of the evening. Perhaps he was beginning to care for her. A little bubble of hope welled up inside her.

She glanced over at Griff several times but could read nothing from his expression. He always managed to keep what he was feeling off his face, while Jolie was afraid everything showed on hers.

They parked the truck and went into the house. Chris was sprawled, sound asleep, on the couch in front of the television.

Griff woke him while Jolie went to check on Riley. He was asleep with his knees drawn up under him and his bottom in the air. He had the wooden animal Chris had brought him clutched in one hand.

Gently she leaned into the crib to kiss him while she pried the carving out of his little fist.

Lost in thought, she headed toward her room, then realized she had not properly thanked Griff for the fun evening. She went back downstairs and found him out on the front porch, leaning on his hands against the rail and staring out over his land.

Jolie came to stand beside him. "I wanted to thank you for tonight. I had a good time."

He didn't say anything for a moment and then he turned and leaned his hips against the rail. He took her arm and pulled her slowly toward him until she stood between the spread of his legs, holding her there with his hands on her shoulders.

The motion set her heart to bumping and she braced her hands on his chest, where she could feel his heart keeping the same speedy rhythm.

He slid his hands up into her hair and slowly brought her face to his, then began to nibble on her lower lip.

She felt a flood of warmth run through her body and tried to think of a reasonable protest, when he stopped nibbling and hauled her in a little closer. His mouth closed over hers, and as his tongue invaded she lost her ability to reason.

He had turned her slightly so she fitted up against him, his arousal against her hip. An answering throb in her own body made her realize they were treading on dangerous ground.

When he finally pulled back and she could take a breath, his words shivered through her.

"The evening doesn't have to end yet." He traced the outside of her ear with his tongue, scattering what little thought she had.

"We're both free, both adults." His hand drifted down her back and up her ribs, brushing the side of her breast. "Come upstairs with me. I've been thinking about you in my bed since you got here."

Oh, how her body yearned for him. She felt as if she was on fire. She shifted her hip and loved the deep groan that rumbled from his chest.

He kissed her again and she swore her toes curled up inside her shoes.

"It's just sex, Jolie. No strings attached. A fun way to end the evening."

He might as well have thrown a bucket of cold water on her. She stiffened and backed away.

No strings. Just fun.

Well, she wanted strings. Wanted to be in love together. Needed to be tied up tight to him.

She wasn't going to settle for less.

Her body screamed at her to say yes. It would be so easy to go with him right now. Find out if all she had been fantasizing about the past few weeks would be as good as she thought.

The practical side of her knew it would make leaving so much harder, and she didn't know how she was going to manage as it was.

She took his face in her palms and gave him a melancholy smile. "I can't. I want to, but I can't. I need more."

His hands dropped away from her body. "I don't have more."

Sadly she kissed his cheek. "I know. I'm not asking. Just telling you what I need."

She turned and went into the house and up the stairs.

He didn't come in for a long time.

The next morning Jolie sat across the breakfast table from Griff. An awkward silence hung between them.

Jolie knew she had to leave. Griff had made his feelings clear.

He wanted sex.

She wanted so much more.

There was no middle ground for them. If she stayed she'd eventually give in and end up in his bed. She was too attracted to him for that not to happen. He made her feel things she'd never felt before.

If she did sleep with him, she wasn't sure she would be able to endure the hurt of leaving.

Griff was doing okay with Riley, and if she wasn't there, he would get closer to the baby.

With an effort she plastered a pleasant expression on her face. "Griff, it's time to look for a permanent nanny for Riley. I need to make plans. My aunt is expecting me."

Griff looked up from his breakfast and fixed her with a hard look. "Is that what you want?"

No, she wanted to scream at him. I love Riley, and I love you. But he didn't want to hear that.

Jolie pushed back her chair and picked up her plate. "It's what we agreed on."

His question made her angry. Did he want her to admit how she felt so he could tell her there was no room in his life for what she wanted?

He brought his plate over to the sink. "What are you mad at?"

She forced a smile and a light tone. "Nothing."

He made an exasperated noise. "Is this about last night? You want me to apologize?"

She'd made him angry. "Of course not. It's time for me to get on with my life."

He stared at her for a moment. "Yes, your life."

"I'll call the paper and place an ad. I'd like to help with the interviewing, if it's okay with you." She was going to make sure whoever he hired was qualified to take care of Riley.

"Fine. It would be best for me if the interviews were at noon or in the evening."

She clutched the edge of the sink. She'd known this

conversation was going to be hard, but she hadn't imagined the pain.

"That shouldn't be too hard to arrange."

He headed for the back door, and as he took his hat and heavy jacket off the hook he said, "Don't fix lunch for me. I'm going to ride fences today."

She watched him cross the yard toward the barn, and when he disappeared inside, she sat down at the kitchen table and put her head down on her crossed arms and had herself a good cry.

"What's the matter with Jolie?" Chris asked.

Griff looked up from the cinch he was tightening with a jerk of fear. "What do you mean? I just left her. She was fine."

"I just came around the side of the house and saw her sitting at the kitchen table. Looked like she was crying."

Why would she be crying? It was her idea to leave. She made it very clear last night she wasn't interested in being anything but Riley's nanny.

"I don't know why she's crying." He led his horse out of the barn.

Chris followed him out. "Are you going to go find out?"

The last thing he wanted was to step into the middle of a crying jag. "Nope."

"Why not?" Chris slapped his hat against the leg of his jeans.

Griff pinned him with a stare. "Don't you have something to do?"

Chris slammed his hat back on his head. "Yup."

"Well, go do it!" He mounted his horse and made a detour up past the house.

The kitchen was empty. She was probably upstairs

getting the baby dressed. He went back over their conversation this morning and couldn't come up with anything he had said that would make her cry.

Hell, he was the one who should be weeping after last night. He'd been so ready to carry her sweet little body upstairs to his bed he'd lain awake aching for her half the night.

He kicked his horse into a canter and shook his head. Women.

Chest aching with unshed tears, Jolie stood at the window holding Riley and watched Griff make a loop toward the house, then turn and ride away.

Jolie kissed the top of Riley's head. "He sure looks good up on that big horse of his."

Riley clapped his hands and crowed, as if in agreement.

She buried her face against the soft skin of his neck and felt the tears threaten again.

His little hands tangled in her hair, and her tears flowed once more.

"Oh, buddy." She sobbed. "What am I going to do without you?"

Chapter Eleven

Jolie stared at her notes on the responses to the ad she'd placed in the paper for a new nanny. The first woman was coming for an interview at noon and the second at twelve-thirty.

Near tears at the thought of leaving Griff and Riley, she wanted to call both of the women back and tell them the ad had been a mistake.

Where was the courage she had been cultivating since she left Seattle?

She could see Griff through the open door of his office, bent over paperwork on his desk. Sun came through the window and gilded his hair the color of gold. She loved Griff and Riley so much after a few weeks. If she stayed, how much more would she love them after months had passed?

How much less would she like herself if she stayed, knowing Griff wanted her in his bed but would never let her into his heart?

Her practical mind told her she had to leave. Her heart gave her a whole different message.

She sighed and turned so she couldn't see Griff. Jolie had put Riley down for an early nap. He was teething and cranky and she didn't want the potential nannies to get a bad first impression.

A car pulled up. Jolie went to the front door.

The heavy-set woman who slowly climbed the steps looked to be in her late forties. Her name was Joan James.

Jolie pasted on a smile and opened the door. Griff came up to stand behind her. "Ms. James?"

The woman nodded.

Jolie extended her hand. "I'm Jolie Carleton. And this is Griff Price."

Ms. James stopped dead on the porch. "You two aren't married? I'm a church-going woman, and I don't hold with living together without marriage."

Jolie took a deep breath and heard Griff groan under his breath. Could they have gotten off to a worse start? Jolie didn't think so.

She opened the door wider and said, "Ms. James, please come in." When the woman didn't budge Jolie added, "I'm Riley's nanny and I'm leaving. You would be my replacement."

Hesitantly she entered the house. What did she want, Jolie thought sourly, a sworn statement that she and Griff had not shared a bed?

"Please, come in and sit down. Tell us about your work experience with children."

She smelled like mothballs.

Gingerly Ms. James lowered herself to the couch and clutched her purse in her lap. "I raised four of my own, so I've had plenty of experience."

Jolie glanced at Griff, whose attention seemed to be fixed on something outside. "I'm sure you have."

An awkward silence fell. Jolie knew this was not the woman to take care of Riley, but she didn't want to be rude and end the interview so abruptly.

Griff was no help at all, staring off into the distance.

She was trying to think of more questions when Ms. James cleared her throat.

"How many hours a week would you need me?"

Jolie thought she had made that very clear in the ad. "It's a live-in position, Ms. James. It would be full-time."

"I have to have Wednesday mornings and Friday afternoons and all day Sunday off."

The only thing Jolie liked about this woman was that she would put a real crimp in Griff's social life if he ever brought a date home.

Griff stood up abruptly. "Well then, Ms. James, I'd say this isn't the job you'd want to take."

Ms. James blinked at him in surprise and then struggled to her feet. With a sniff she said, "I suppose it isn't."

Griff walked her to the door and thanked her for coming. When she made it to her car, he closed the door and turned to Jolie.

She eyed him for a moment. "You were very abrupt."

He shrugged. "No use wasting her time or ours. You knew right away she wasn't the one."

Jolie smiled. "Yes. Pretty much when she first opened her mouth."

"When's the next one due?"

"In about fifteen minutes."

The end of Jolie's sentence was drowned out by the ringing of Griff's cell phone. He dug the phone out of his pocket, gave his usual terse greeting, listened for a moment, then said, "I'll be right there."

Jolie raised a brow in question.

"I've got a mare down in the barn. Will you handle the next interview by yourself?"

"I can. But we haven't talked about what you're looking for."

He studied her face for a minute, and in a low voice he said, "That's easy. I want someone just like you."

He turned and walked through the dining room into the kitchen.

Jolie heard the screen door slam behind him. Someone just like her? What did he mean by that?

She didn't have time to give his statement more thought as a rusty old VW bug pulled up in front of the house.

She watched a young woman with long red hair dressed in a tight, cropped stretch top and shorts unroll herself from the driver's seat.

This would be Kimberley McKenzie. What was the girl thinking, dressed like that? It was close to freezing outside.

As Miss McKenzie jogged up the front steps Jolie noticed two things at once. The girl wasn't wearing a bra and she had a tattoo peeking out of the waistband of her shorts.

And she was very, very attractive.

Jolie took a deep breath and vowed to be objective. She opened the door as Miss McKenzie crossed the porch.

"Miss McKenzie?"

"Yeah. Call me Kimmie." She smiled.

"I'm Jolie Carleton. Please come in."

Kimmie looked around the room with great interest. "This is a way cool house."

Jolie nodded. "Please sit down." She gestured to the couch and noticed a toe ring on Kimmie's left foot and wondered how many points she should deduct for not dressing properly for a job interview.

"Tell me about your experience with children, Kimmie."

Kimmie rolled her eyes and gestured widely. "I'm the oldest of seven. I got stuck taking care of my brothers and sisters all my life."

"Why do you want a job in child care?"

"It's live-in, right? I like, want to move away from home, and I figure it will be easy to take care of one kid."

"How old are you?"

"I'm like, nineteen. I graduated high school last June."

"Won't you get lonely out here with no friends and no social life?"

Kimmie shrugged. "My friends can come here. I mean, it'll be like, okay, won't it, to have friends here?"

Jolie knew how much Griff enjoyed his quiet evenings after working hard all day. "You'd have to discuss that with Mr. Price."

Kimmie nodded and tore at a loose piece of skin around her thumb nail.

"Do you have any questions, Kimmie?"

"Yeah. Does Mr. Price have satellite TV?"

Jolie stood up. "No, I'm afraid not. Any other questions?"

Kimmie shook her head and got to her feet.

Jolie walked her to the door. "I'll give you a call. We still have another candidate to interview."

"Sure. Whatever. Thanks." Kimmie bounced down the stairs, got in her car and sped away in a cloud of dust without fastening her seat belt.

Jolie stared at the retreating car. Unless the next candidate was a child-eating monster, Kimmie was out of luck.

How was she going to find someone she thought was qualified to take care of Riley? Who would love him the way he needed and deserved to be loved?

She knew Kimmie wasn't qualified, but would she know if someone was?

Jolie sank down on the couch. Maybe she should stay. Was she being foolish to give up Riley because Griff wouldn't make a commitment?

Jolie knew the answer was no. It might be okay for a while, but she would always want more. If she stayed now, she knew she'd end up in Griff's bed. She reminded herself for the second time in an hour that leaving would be just that much harder down the road.

She loved him. Loved him so much she wanted marriage and children and the whole package. She wasn't going to settle for less.

Her mantra was live with courage, and she had to follow through. She would find a new nanny and get on with her life.

Griff finished rubbing Honeygirl down, covered her with a blanket and turned her into a stall.

"Stan, if she goes down again, call me. I'm going up to the house."

"Sure thing, boss."

Griff handed Stan the cloth he'd been using and shrugged into his jacket before heading out of the barn. Maybe he could catch the end of the second interview.

He'd promised Jolie he'd help with them even though he wasn't sure what questions to ask, let alone the right answers.

They wouldn't even have to do this if Jolie would agree to stay. He knew she loved the kid and there certainly was attraction between the two of them.

He'd lain awake half the night again thinking about the fact that she was sleeping just down the hall. But she wanted something from him that he didn't have to give.

He'd been married, and the fairy tale he suspected Jolie wanted didn't exist. He knew this from firsthand experience.

He shoved open the back door, threw his hat onto a hook and shrugged out of his jacket. Deirdre had cured him of believing in the possibility of happy-ever-after.

He found Jolie sitting in the living room staring out the window.

"Did the second one show up?"

Jolie shot him a sour look. "Oh, yes. She was not suitable."

"What do you mean, not suitable? Why?"

"A teenager looking to move away from home."

Jolie looked as tired as he felt. He wondered if she'd been as sleepless as he had before he pulled himself back to the conversation. "And that makes her unsuitable?"

"Her big questions were did you have a satellite dish and could her friends come over. She didn't ask one question about the baby."

"I see."

"I'm not sure you do."

Her hard tone surprised him, and before he could say anything she started talking.

"Riley needs to be loved as much as he needs to be

taken care of. He's made so much progress. You can't just hire anyone. You need someone who understands him. Someone who's patient and kind and…and…"

She seemed to run out of steam, and tears overflowed and ran down her cheeks.

Awkwardly Griff sat down beside her and put his arms around her, pulling her up against his chest. Tears always unnerved him.

He murmured into her hair. "He needs you. Stay here." It's what she wanted, and certainly what he wanted.

Jolie pushed away and wiped at her cheeks with her sleeve. "You know that won't work. We both want things the other person isn't willing to give. If I stayed we'd end up hating each other."

Griff couldn't imagine ever hating Jolie. But she was right, she did want what he couldn't give.

He cupped her chin and brought her head up so he could see her face. "I wish you'd change your mind."

Fresh tears welled up in her eyes. "I wish I could."

Sounds of Riley waking up from his nap drifted downstairs, and they both turned their heads toward the stairs. Jolie started to get up, and Griff gently pushed her back on the couch.

"I'll get him. You look tired." He didn't miss the surprise on her face. He knew he hadn't been pulling his weight where the boy was concerned. It was time he pitched in more.

She raised one eyebrow. "All right, but he'll need his diaper changed."

Hell, if he could muck out stalls he could handle a diaper. "No problem. Put your feet up for a while."

He was aware of her eyes on him all the way up the stairs. There was another woman who'd answered their

ad. She was coming tonight after supper. Perhaps if she
didn't work out, he could talk Jolie into staying for a
while.

He knew she would put Riley's well-being above everything else. He wasn't above using that to get her to
stay. He wanted her here even on her terms. He didn't
want to face her leaving.

Jolie promised herself a few moments to rest and to
give Griff time with Riley. The next thing she knew, he
was shaking her shoulder to tell her supper was ready.

She sat up and rubbed her eyes. "Where's Riley?"

"He's in his high chair eating."

"I didn't mean to fall asleep." She glanced at the
clock on the mantel. To her surprise she'd slept two
hours.

"Well, I guess you needed it. Come on."

He held out his hand and pulled her to her feet. "We
need to eat before the last interview comes."

The last interview. She'd forgotten. A Mrs. Muller
was driving out in an hour. She smoothed her hair and
followed Griff to the kitchen.

Riley waved when she came through the door, a hunk
of banana in one hand and part of a squashed peanut
butter sandwich in the other.

"Hey, buddy. You eating dinner?"

Riley babbled a reply and offered her a bite of his
sandwich. "Thank you, sweetheart, but I have my own
dinner right here."

She pulled the high chair closer to the table and sat
down to mugs of soup and sandwiches.

"Sorry I slept so long."

Griff just shrugged. "No problem. We guys managed
to get along." He began to eat.

It should make her feel better that they could get along, but instead she felt tears threaten again. She didn't want them to get along without her. She wanted to be part of them.

They ate in silence. Even Riley was quiet, as if he sensed their somber mood.

When they finished, Griff went into his office, and Jolie cleaned up supper and Riley, then got him into his pajamas.

As she was coming down the stairs she heard a knock on the front door. "I'll get it."

Jolie, Riley perched on her hip, opened the front door.

A pleasant-looking woman in her fifties smiled at Jolie. "Hello. I'm Alice Muller."

"Come in, please. I'm Jolie Carleton, and this is Riley Price." She stepped back to let Mrs. Muller in.

The older woman bent down until she was eye level with Riley. "Hello, Riley."

Riley ducked his head against Jolie's chest. "He's a little shy with new people."

Mrs. Muller smiled and straightened up. "Most children are."

Griff came into the living room, and Jolie introduced them and suggested they all sit.

She explained what the job required, and Mrs. Muller talked about her background and experience. As Jolie listened, she decided that Mrs. Muller was perfect for the job. Sadly she studied the woman who would probably be taking care of Riley.

Griff spoke up. "Why are you leaving your current position?"

Mrs. Muller teared up. "I'm sorry. It's just that I've been with the same family since their eldest child was born, almost eight years. The company they both work

for is moving them to southern California. I don't want
to move away. My own children and grandchildren live
right here in Billings and Acton.''

Jolie liked this woman. Mrs. Muller seemed to have
her priorities straight. "Would you mind giving us your
employer's name and telephone number as a reference?''

"Of course.'' Mrs. Muller pulled a tablet out of her
purse and jotted down the information, handing the slip
to Griff.

They all stood up with the awkwardness of ending the
interview, and Jolie asked one last question. "When
would you be free?''

"I promised I would help with the packing, so not
until Saturday.''

Jolie nodded, and as they walked to the door she
thanked Mrs. Muller for coming.

Saturday. She laid her cheek on top of Riley's head.

That was four days away.

Chapter Twelve

Jolie took all the clothes out of the second drawer in Riley's dresser and measured the new drawer liner. Mrs. Muller's references had been glowing, and Griff had offered her the job. Now Jolie had three days to pack and get the house in shape before she left.

She glanced back at Riley as she finished putting the clothes back over the fresh liner. He was sitting in the middle of the floor, chewing on the trunk of a stuffed elephant and drooling down the front of his shirt.

She made a mental note to tell Mrs. Muller that he was teething, then had to will back a fresh wave of tears the thought of leaving him always brought.

She studied the contents of the next drawer. She wanted to leave Griff's home in tip-top condition for the new nanny. And perhaps by keeping busy she would tire herself out and be able to sleep tonight.

Her stomach growled, and she realized it was time for lunch. At breakfast Griff had mentioned something about not being home midday because they were moving cows closer before the weather got bad.

There had been a few snow flurries yesterday afternoon, but not enough to stick to the ground. If it snowed in the next two days she and Riley could build his first snowman.

Jolie scooped Riley off the floor and nuzzled his neck, drinking in the fresh baby smell of him. He squealed and grabbed for her hair. "You hungry, buddy? How about lunch?"

She perched him on her hip and carried him down to the kitchen, putting him in his high chair.

The back door slammed and her heart skipped a beat. Maybe Griff had changed his plans and come home. But when she looked up, there was no one there.

Disappointed, she realized the wind must have caught the door. She went out and pulled it firmly closed.

Griff. Her mind knew she'd made the right decision, but her heart refused to go along. She stood and stared as leaves danced and skipped across the yard. The porch was cold, as if the temperature had dipped since this morning.

Jolie closed the door between the porch and the kitchen. "Maybe we can take a walk after lunch, buddy, before your nap."

She sat at the kitchen table and spread peanut butter and jelly on a slice of bread and cut half of it in quarters for Riley and munched on the other half herself.

Riley tossed the last piece of his sandwich on the floor, his new signal he was finished eating.

"All done?"

She wiped his hands and face while he wiggled and squirmed, then lifted him down and sat him in the middle of the floor with his favorite wooden spoon and a saucepan.

"I'm going to get our jackets and then we can go outside." Riley banged the spoon against the side of the pan and crowed like a rooster.

Jolie went to the hall closet and grabbed up their jackets. When she came back around the corner into the kitchen, to her horror Riley was standing unsteadily on the seat of a kitchen chair. In the short time she'd been gone, he'd managed to climb onto the chair.

"Riley!" she yelled, and knew immediately she had made a terrible mistake.

He turned to look at her and lost his balance.

Everything seemed to go in slow motion as she lunged across the room. He toppled off the chair and bounced against the edge of the kitchen table before he landed on the floor.

For a split second he was utterly quiet, and then he began to wail like a banshee. Trembling, Jolie scooped him up from the floor and hugged him against her chest, cradling his head and crooning soothing words to him.

His little body shook with his sobs, and Jolie felt so guilty for leaving him to get the jackets she wanted to cry right along with him.

"I'm sorry, buddy. I'm so sorry. I know you're scared. I'm right here." She rocked him against her, and still he sobbed. She could feel his warm tears soaking through her top.

When he didn't quiet down after a few minutes she pulled him away from her chest in order to get a closer look at him.

His little face was covered with blood.

Her legs turned rubbery, and she sat down with a

thump on one of the kitchen chairs, fear churning in her belly. "Oh, no. Oh, baby, I'm so sorry."

She grabbed a napkin off the table and tried to blot Riley's head so she could see how badly he was cut, and he screamed even louder.

"Okay, okay, I know it hurts, but I have to look." Panicked, she didn't know how to deal with this.

Everything she had ever learned about first aid flew right out of her head. She took some deep breaths to try to calm herself. Suddenly she remembered she needed to put pressure on the cut.

When she pressed on the wound, Riley arched his back and threw his arms wide with such force she nearly lost her grip on him.

She carried the still-howling child over to the wall phone. With shaking fingers she punched in Griff's cell phone number.

After two rings that seemed to take forever, she got a recorded message his telephone was not on and invited her to leave a message.

She waited for the tone and asked him to come to the house as soon as he could. As she hung up she wondered if he would be able to understand her over Riley's cries.

Jolie grabbed a clean kitchen towel and sat back down at the table. Again she tried to find the source of all the blood while Riley frantically attempted to push her hands out of the way.

She found the gash up near his hairline, and the size of it made her nauseous. Surely he needed stitches and X-rays. He'd also split his lip, but even though it had puffed up to twice its normal size and bled freely it didn't worry her nearly as much as the head wound.

Trembling, Jolie went to the phone again and dialed

the bunkhouse. Chris or Lem could drive them into Billings.

The Mexican cook answered the telephone. When she asked for Chris or Lem, his only answer was "No here."

She knew he spoke little English and she had no Spanish. Then she remembered all the hands were with Griff, helping him move the cows.

Jolie grabbed a fresh towel, wrapped an ice cube in the corner and pressed it against the gash, but the blood still flowed.

What if he had a concussion? Or a fractured skull?

"Oh, sweety, I'm going to drive into Billings. The hospital emergency room is across the street from your pediatrician's office, so we know the way." She was chattering at him as much to soothe herself as to quiet him.

With shaking hands she bundled the still-crying baby into his jacket, then, holding him, awkwardly slipped into her own. After grabbing a fresh towel and her purse, she carried him to the back door.

At first she thought the door was stuck, then she realized the wind was blowing against the house making the door difficult to push open.

His car seat was in her car. She loaded Riley in and kissed his hair. The bleeding had slowed and a goose egg was already forming on his forehead, but his wails had subsided to occasional sobs and watery hiccups.

As they headed out to the main road, she kept searching the open land, hoping to spot Griff or one of the hands. Flurries of snow made it difficult to see very far, and what she could see was deserted.

She would feel better if someone else was driving and she could sit in the back with Riley. He was settling down a bit, but she could see in her rearview mirror that his head was still bleeding.

Maybe she should have called 911. Immediately she dismissed the thought. An ambulance would have to come from Billings and would take almost as long to get to the ranch as it would for her to drive in.

The snow seemed heavier, and she slowed down a bit and turned on her headlights. It was getting harder to see the road. She tried to determine if she was driving into the storm, or if it was coming from behind her. The swirling winds made it impossible to tell.

Riley's cries had stopped. Jolie glanced in her rearview mirror. The baby's head was nodding. Frantically she tried to think if she was supposed to keep him awake after a blow to the head, or if it was okay to let him sleep.

Should she pull over and try to wake him? Or would it be better to just push thorough to Billings? If she stopped and woke him, he'd just fall asleep again as soon as they got started.

"I'll keep going. The quicker we get to Billings the better." Somehow it made her feel better to talk out loud. She didn't feel so alone.

She could barely see the road. She slowed more and wished she had checked the odometer before they left the house. She had no idea how far they had come, and the snow made everything seem out of focus.

She glanced back at Riley. He was sound asleep. At least, she hoped he was asleep.

Her own breath caught on a worried sob.

She turned her attention back to the road and saw headlights headed right for her. She pulled her steering wheel to the right with a hard jerk.

Her car bounced up over the shoulder and then jolted

nose down, throwing her to the left. She smacked her head against the door frame. A white bolt of pain shot through her head, then faded into black.

Griff felt his horse shudder under him as he flipped up his jacket collar and turned his back to the howling wind. They had managed to move most of the herd, and he could only hope the other steers were trailing behind. He couldn't see ten feet.

The storm had turned much worse than he'd expected, and he was relieved to have the animals closer in, in case he had to deliver feed to them.

He cupped his gloved hands to his mouth and hollered to the men closest to him to spread the word to head in.

Given her head, Honeygirl headed toward the barn. He planned to eat at the cookshack with his hands. He'd told Jolie he wouldn't be there for lunch. To be honest, he had to admit he'd been staying away. Things between them were very awkward.

Relieved to be out of the howling wind, as soon as he made it to the barn he stripped off his gloves. As he unsaddled his horse he realized his phone was beeping, signaling he had a message. The wind had been so fierce he hadn't heard the signal.

He punched in his code and listened to Jolie's frantic message that he come home, with the baby wailing in the background.

Griff ran toward the house. Jolie's car was gone, and the back door was open, the screen banging against the door frame in the wind.

He raced into the kitchen and stopped dead. There were bloody towels on the kitchen table, along with a cutting board and a knife.

She'd hurt herself. His gut twisted at the thought. He

ran through the downstairs, calling her name. Maybe she'd moved her car inside before the storm hit and she was still here.

He took the stairs two at a time. She and the baby were both gone. Of course she'd taken Riley. She'd never leave him here by himself.

Griff raced back down the stairs and fought the wind out to the tractor barn. His truck was there, but Jolie's car was gone.

She should have waited for him. She probably didn't have any experience driving in a blizzard.

Fear seized him.

He jumped in his truck and drove to the cookshack. The men were filling cups with steaming coffee and gathering around the woodstove. Steam rose off their damp clothing.

"Chris, Lem, get your jackets. Jolie's hurt and she went out in the storm."

"What do you mean hurt, boss?" Chris asked.

"She left a message on my phone and there are bloody towels on the kitchen table. She must be driving herself into Billings."

"Riley?"

"She took him with her. There was nobody here to watch him."

Chris and Lem grabbed their jackets off the pegs by the door.

"We've got to find her." If only he'd checked his telephone sooner.

Lem caught his arm as he opened the door. "Boss, let's call the hospital. See if she's already there. She could have made it in."

Griff appreciated Lem's cool thinking. "Good idea.

And the state troopers. They can be checking the road, too.''

He handed Lem his phone as they piled into the truck. Before they made the main road, Lem had reached the hospital and determined that Jolie had not arrived.

Next he called the state troopers and explained the situation. They promised to dispatch a unit from Billings and work out toward the ranch.

The snow seemed to be letting up a bit. They turned toward Billings and crawled down the highway. Any tire tracks had long been covered by the snowfall.

Chris reached out and laid a hand on Griff's sleeve. ''What? Did you see something?''

''No, boss. Sorry. Why don't you let me drive?''

''No. I got it.'' He'd go crazy if he didn't have something to do with his hands.

''Let me know if you change your mind.''

He nodded. ''Lem, try the hospital again. Give them my cell number. If she comes in, have them call us.''

''Okay, boss.''

Griff listened to Lem place the call and leave the message with a growing sense of dread.

If she hadn't made it to Billings and had had an accident, how long could she and the baby survive in this bitter cold?

Jolie wasn't from around here. She didn't realize how storms like this could blow in with little or no warning.

He should have told her, warned her.

Griff and Chris both spotted the faint red flash of a hazard light in the ditch beside the road.

Griff skidded to a halt and backed up as Chris opened the door and leaped from the truck.

Griff was around the side and sliding down into the

ditch beside the disabled car as Lem came flying out from the back seat.

The car had settled against the bank on the driver's side. The windows were covered with a heavy coating of snow. The three men dug frantically to clear the back door so they could get into the vehicle.

When they had cleared enough snow to drag open the door, Griff found Jolie huddled motionless on the back seat. She had her body curled against the back of the seat.

For a terrible moment fear held him frozen in place.

Jolie wasn't moving, and there was no sign of the baby.

Where was the baby? Where was Riley?

Griff slid into the car and touched a hand to Jolie's shoulder. "Jolie, sweetheart? Wake up." She didn't move, and Griff felt a ball of ice form in his gut.

He didn't want to shake her. She could be badly injured. He peeled off a glove and ran his hand up under her hair to the back of her neck. To his relief he could feel her pulse and her skin was warm to his touch.

"Jolie, can you hear me?"

She groaned and tried to sit up.

"Don't move yet." He held her down with a gentle pressure on her shoulder.

"Jolie, where's the baby, honey?"

Her voice sounded muffled against the seat. "Inside my jacket. I got in the back to keep him warm."

Griff felt a flood of relief. He turned toward the two anxious faces of his hands. "Lem, there's a blanket behind the back seat in my truck."

Lem nodded and scrambled up the embankment.

Griff turned back to Jolie. "Does your neck hurt? Or your back?"

She was quiet for a moment. "No, just my head."

"All right. I want you to see if you can sit up. Take it slow." He gripped her shoulders and helped her into a sitting position. It was awkward going, because of the tilt of the car.

The left side of her face was bloody.

She was clutching her jacket around the baby. Her gloveless hands were blue.

"Is Riley hurt?"

"I think he's asleep."

"Let me have him, sweetheart."

She looked at him as if she was trying to figure out who he was. "I was taking him to the hospital." She didn't seem to want to let go of the baby.

Griff pried one of her hands loose and managed to lift Riley out of her arms. He was breathing regularly, but his little face was smeared with dried blood.

Griff rubbed his cold hand over the baby's cheek, and he woke up with a whimper, then grinned up at Griff.

He held him against his chest. "Thank God," he whispered into the toddler's matted hair.

Gently Griff handed Riley over to Chris. "Take him up in the cab and keep him warm.

He helped Jolie scoot toward the door. "Let's see if you can stand up." Her whole body was trembling.

She clutched at his arm. "Where's Riley?"

"Chris took him to my truck. It's warm in the cab."

"Warm?" She said longingly as he draped the blanket around her shoulders.

"We'll get you up there right now." He angled her legs out of the car. "You need to stand up."

"Okay."

He helped her upright, and her knees buckled under her. Griff picked her up, but he knew he'd have a hard time getting up the steep bank with her.

Lem hovered at his elbow, then turned and pointed

back along the road. "Boss, the bank isn't as steep back this way."

With Lem's help he made it up to the highway just as a trooper pulled to a stop. He made a U-turn to park behind Griff's truck.

He climbed out of his cruiser. "Need an ambulance?"

Griff held Jolie's welcome weight against his chest. "It will be quicker to take them in ourselves."

The trooper eyed her. "Is she badly hurt?"

"No, I don't think so." Griff prayed he was right as he kept walking toward his truck.

The trooper yelled after him. "Is anyone else in the car?"

Lem answered for Griff. "Nope."

As Griff handed Jolie into the back seat of the cab, the trooper came up behind him. "I'll call for a wrecker and have the car towed. Where do you want it to go?"

Griff didn't give a damn about the car. "Have him take it to Winslow's."

"Will do. You drive carefully now. You'll probably meet the plow in another few miles."

Griff climbed in beside Jolie and scooped her onto his lap. Chris and Lem were already in the front, and Jolie insisted they hand the baby back to her.

Jolie settled the baby against her chest, and Griff held them both all the way into Billings.

He'd never been so scared in his life.

When they pulled up outside the emergency room, Griff coaxed Jolie into handing the baby over to a waiting nurse, then bundled her into a wheelchair. An orderly took her off to the X-ray department.

He held Riley while the doctor examined the gash on the child's head and applied sterile strips to the cut.

A nurse came in and cleaned off the dried blood on

Riley's face. She gave Griff instructions on keeping the area dry for a few days, then pronounced them released.

Griff hoisted Riley onto his hip and went in search of Jolie. He spotted Chris talking to a pretty little brunette nurse in a corner of the waiting room.

After questioning several people, he found Jolie in a bed in an exam cubicle, arguing with the doctor, who was looking at a set of X-rays on the light box on the wall.

"I feel fine, really. I don't want to spend the night."

She was pale, setting off the livid bruise that surrounded the cut on her temple.

Riley and Jolie were going to have matching black eyes.

Her left wrist was in a brace and two fingers on her right hand were splinted.

The doctor eyed her over the top of his glasses. "You have a concussion. You need to stay for observation."

She spotted Griff in the doorway, her worried eyes on Riley. "Is he okay?"

Griff moved closer to the bed. "Doctor said he's fine. Didn't even put in stitches."

Eyes filled with tears, she reached for Riley as the baby held out his arms to her. "Griff, I don't want to stay here."

God, he wanted to take her home and hold her all night. But the doctor was right.

Griff cleared his throat. "You heard what the doctor said. Just for one night." Then he'd bring her home and hold her all night.

"Listen to your husband. It's only one night." He gestured to Riley and then Griff as he headed toward the door. "These fellows can get along without you for that long. That painkiller is going to make you sleep in a few minutes."

Husband, Griff thought as he nodded in agreement with the doctor. A month ago the label would have had him running like a spooked steer. Now it didn't sound so bad.

Jolie looked as if she was going to argue further, then she seemed to give up and close her eyes.

Griff lifted Riley out of her limp arms. He bent down and kissed her forehead. "You sleep, darlin', and I'll pick you up first thing tomorrow."

Her eyes fluttered open and she mumbled, "Promise. First thing. Bring me some clothes, okay?"

"You bet. We'll see you tomorrow." He kissed her again but she was already asleep.

Griff caught up with the doctor. "She's going to be okay, right?"

"She'll have a headache for a few days. The sprained wrist should be rested. The two broken fingers will probably be the worst of it, especially dealing with this little guy." He lifted Riley's chin to look at the gash on his head.

The baby pulled back. Griff laughed. "I think he's had enough poking for one day."

"Can you get your wife some help with the baby?"

"Sure. Thanks, Doc." He'd call Alice Muller as soon as he got home and ask her to start working early. If she couldn't, he'd stay home.

He went out and collected Lem and Chris. They stopped by the garage to get the baby's car seat and then headed back to the Circle P.

Griff glanced down at his watch, amazed that it was only four in the afternoon. It felt like the longest day of his life.

Chapter Thirteen

Jolie came awake and tried to shift into a comfortable position on the narrow hospital bed. In spite of the pain medication the nurse had given her, every part of her body ached, her head most of all.

She cracked open one eye and saw a tall figure standing at the window surrounded by the early glow of dawn.

Her heart gave a little leap. Griff had come to take her home.

Then she realized it wasn't Griff.

"Daddy?" She saw him turn with a start.

"Baby, how are you feeling?" He crossed the room and sat on the chair beside the bed.

She groaned. "Oh, don't ask. I had a really bad day yesterday."

"So I heard. What were you thinking, driving into a blizzard?"

Jolie closed her eyes and fought back the tears. She knew her father loved her, but he still treated her like a nine-year-old with no sense.

"There was an emergency." She didn't have the energy to explain, and he would just argue with her until he declared himself the winner.

She changed the subject. "How did you find out about the accident?"

"The man who owns the ranch where you've been staying gave me a call last night."

"Griff?"

He nodded. "So I left right away. As soon as you are released this morning we can fly back to Seattle."

"But my car—"

"Will be shipped. And Mr. Price will send your things."

"You spoke to him?"

"I left a message." He said it as if it never occurred to him his request could be denied.

Jolie closed her eyes and let the tears come. As easily as that, Griff would pack up her belongings. Would he be able to pack away his memories, as well? She almost laughed at the romantic thought. She suspected the memories were very one-sided in their relationship.

Maybe it was for the best that she leave today and make a clean break. Every day she stayed she fell more in love with Griff and Riley, making the prospect of saying goodbye more difficult.

Courage, she told herself. You've been practicing for weeks. Have courage.

She counted up the reasons she should leave. The new nanny would be ready to start tomorrow or the next day. Perhaps it would be good for Griff and Riley to be together without her to act as a go-between until the woman could start.

She couldn't take care of Riley very well with a brace on one wrist and splints on two of her fingers.

"Jolie? Are you in pain? Should I call the nurse?"

She used the sheet to wipe her face. "Some. I'm mostly tired."

She suspected the pain she felt now had no cure but time.

Obviously uncomfortable, her father said, "I'll go see if I can hurry up the discharge procedure."

Of course he would, Jolie thought as her father strode out of her room. Richard Carleton had a way of making people jump.

She eased herself out of bed and walked hunched over like an old lady to the bathroom. As she washed her hands, she glanced into the mirror above the sink. She didn't recognize her own face. Swollen and bruised, both her eyes were blackened.

Shaken by how bad she looked, she got back into bed. She fumbled with the telephone and dialed Griff's number without having a clear idea of how she would say goodbye.

The answering machine picked up and she replaced the receiver without leaving a message. Even though she wasn't sure what she would say, she didn't want to leave it on his machine.

A doctor she had not seen before came in and stood at the foot of her bed. "Good morning, Miss Carleton."

Is it? She wanted to ask him. It didn't feel the least bit good to her.

He was looking at the chart in his hand and didn't seem to notice that she hadn't answered him. He asked a few questions about the severity of her headache, then nodded and left.

She tried Griff again at home and on his cell phone and didn't get an answer on either.

Her door opened. She hoped to see Griff, but it was

the nurse this time. She held a tiny plastic cup containing three pills.

Jolie looked dubious as she stared at the medication. "What are these for?"

The nurse smiled and poured her a glass of water from the pitcher beside the bed. "Doctor changed your pain medication. A prescription is being filled right now for you to take with you."

Jolie swallowed the pills under the watchful eye of the nurse, then lay back and closed her eyes against the pounding in her temples.

As soon as the painkiller took effect, she'd try Griff again.

She was jostled awake as a nurse and an orderly lifted her into a wheelchair. Her muzzy brain tried to get hold of a reason.

"More tests?" she asked. Her tongue felt thick and slow.

"No, no more tests. You're being released."

Released? But she hadn't spoken to Griff yet. The corridor seemed to tilt and spin as they wheeled her to the elevator.

When the elevator doors opened, her father was standing there waiting for her. It took her a moment to remember he had flown in.

She struggled to gather her wits. "Daddy, I need to make a call."

"You can do that from the plane. There's another storm coming down from Canada, and we need to take off before it hits."

She couldn't seem to clear her head long enough to come up with an answer, so she let them help her into the car and belt her in as if she were a child.

* * *

Griff had Riley on one arm and a huge bouquet of sunflowers in the other. He had called the hospital before dawn. Jolie spent a comfortable night. He didn't know how she could possibly be comfortable as banged up as she was, but they assured him she could be released today.

He'd had trouble sleeping all night. Every time he dozed off he'd awakened with dreams of searching for Jolie and the baby and not being able to find them.

About three-thirty he'd made a decision. He was going to ask her to stay. There were things they needed to work out, but they were two reasonable adults. Surely they could come to some kind of arrangement.

He didn't want to think of a future without her.

Between feeding Riley breakfast and wrestling him into his clothes and diaper changes, it had taken a lot longer than he thought it would to get himself and the baby ready to go.

He stopped outside Jolie's door and took a deep breath. He needed the most important words of his life right now, and he wasn't sure what he was going to say.

He hoisted Riley higher on his hip. "Back me up, buddy. I'm asking for both of us."

Riley gave him a drooly grin, showing off his new teeth.

Griff pushed the door open. Jolie's bed was empty, stripped of bedding. Griff felt a bolt of fear that something had happened, then got ahold of himself. They probably moved her to another room.

Heart pounding in his chest, he approached a nurse carrying a tray of supplies.

"Excuse me, where did you move Miss Carleton?"

She raised her eyebrows and said, "Miss Carleton was released a half hour ago."

Released? "Where did she go?" She didn't have a ride to the ranch.

"Her father came and got her. They're flying back to Seattle."

He'd spoken to her father last night. Mr. Carleton hadn't said he was coming to Billings. "Do you know which airline?" He could catch them at the airport.

"I believe he has his own plane. He hired a private-duty nurse to go along."

"I see. Thanks." Griff turned and walked back down the corridor.

She'd left without even bothering to call. He shoved the flowers into a trash can by the nurse's station.

"Come on, Riley. It's time to go home."

Jolie got through Christmas and the New Year holidays by sheer will. She used the bruising on her face and the cast on her wrist as an excuse to avoid most of the social gatherings she usually attended this time of year.

She sent Riley a box of toys with a card for Griff. She'd wanted to find a box big enough to send herself.

After returning to Seattle she spent several days in the hospital at her father's insistence. Further X-rays had indicated a broken bone in her wrist rather than a simple sprain.

Finally home, she answered every telephone call that came to the house and checked the mail every day hoping to hear from Griff.

Then, after two weeks, the ritual became too painful and she stopped.

The one thing that kept her going was the foundation she started, an idea that came to her while she lay in the hospital. She used a portion of her trust fund to get it going, then threw herself into learning to write for grants and other funding to keep it afloat.

Her vision was simple. An organization of volunteer advocates who would speak out for children caught up in the foster care system. Children like Riley, who were not lucky enough to have family take them in, who got lost in the shuffle of a system where social workers were overworked and the courts jammed with cases. The children inevitably suffered.

The organizing kept her busy, but couldn't keep her thoughts from wandering to a ranch in Montana where the two people she loved most lived.

Perhaps time healed all wounds, but it seemed to Jolie that the hole in her heart was getting bigger instead of smaller.

Chapter Fourteen

Griff hung up the telephone, then stared out the window of his office at the blanket of snow that had fallen last night. Winslow's Garage was ready to ship Jolie's car back to Seattle.

What the hell was the matter with him? Before the call he'd been sitting hunched over his account books for more than an hour and had accomplished nothing. Now he was staring out the window.

The ranch was running well. Alice, the new nanny, was taking great care of Riley and the house, and he was pushing himself through each day, hoping to be tired enough to sleep at night.

He slid the Christmas card from Jolie from under the blotter on his desk. She had written him an impersonal little note and included it with a box of toys for Riley.

He'd read it a thousand times.

Maybe a cup of coffee might help clear his head. He walked into the kitchen as the new nanny was wiping breakfast off Riley's face.

Alice Muller looked up. "Coffee? Fresh pot."

She was wonderful. Quietly efficient, good cook, and she never pried into his personal life.

Everything he'd thought he wanted.

He missed Jolie so badly it hurt.

Riley, tired of being ignored, squealed and held out his arms to Griff.

Griff felt a little twist in the middle of his chest. When had he become so attached to the child? The little fellow had wormed his way into Griff's heart.

"Hey, buddy," he said, using Jolie's favorite nickname for the boy. "You finally done eating?"

He lifted Riley out of the high chair and set him on the floor. He wobbled and grabbed hold of Griff's leg.

"Alice, where did you put Miss Carleton's suitcase?" He would drop it off at Winslow's this afternoon so it could be shipped with her car.

"In the closet in the baby's room."

Griff had asked Alice to pack up Jolie's things. He had been so angry when she'd left so suddenly, he didn't want to deal with it.

"Her car is repaired, so I'm going to take her bag into Billings later. It can be shipped with the car." And then he wouldn't have a physical reminder of her in the house.

Yeah, Price, he thought. No physical reminders, just memories that haunted him awake and asleep.

He picked up Riley and handed him to Alice so he wouldn't try to follow Griff out the back door and down to the barns.

Ranch work had slowed to a crawl, and Griff hadn't replaced the two hands who had quit around Christmas. He had enough work for those who were left until he had to hire again in the spring.

He found Chris and Lem in the tractor barn. The engine of the thresher was spread out on an old blanket on the floor.

"Find the problem yet?" He eyed the parts with a degree of skepticism. Things mechanical were beyond him.

Chris looked up. "Yeah, I think we found the problem."

"I'm going in to Winslow's. You need him to order parts?"

"If it's what we think, we're okay." Chris bent back over his work, then looked up. "You going to get Miss Jolie's car? Is she coming to pick it up?"

"No. Winslow's going to ship it to Seattle."

Chris looked disappointed. "Too bad."

Griff turned abruptly and walked out, not knowing if Chris was referring to Jolie or the car.

The thought of her coming back brought a yearning he didn't want to deal with.

Griff headed back to the house and shucked off his jacket and hat on the mud porch. Alice was up to her elbows in flour when he walked into the kitchen.

"Where's Riley?"

"Down for his morning nap. I put the suitcase out in the hall." She gestured to a small pile of folded clothes on the counter. "You need to put those away."

He didn't recognize the clothes. "What are these?"

"I found them in a basket of clean baby clothes. I assume they belong to Miss Carleton."

Grabbing the clothes, he headed upstairs and picked up Jolie's leather bag on the way to his room.

He put the suitcase on the bed and snapped open the latches. When he raised the lid Jolie's scent wafted up and nearly brought him to his knees.

Bracing both hands on the edge of the bed, he stared at Jolie's things. He'd made a huge mistake. Jolie wasn't Deirdre. Or his mother. He had lumped all women together and lost his chance with her because of it.

When she'd first arrived he'd tagged her as a woman running from a man. The way his wife had run and his mother.

But Jolie had proved her staying power. No matter how he had pulled away in the beginning, she'd pushed and pushed until he'd gotten used to Riley. He'd stopped seeing the boy as a symbol of the betrayal of his wife and brother.

That alone was a gift he could never repay.

He'd pressured her for a physical relationship with no strings attached, and even though she'd been tempted, she'd stuck by her guns.

Jolie might have grown up soft and pampered, but she'd shown him a strong woman. She had honesty. And character.

She wanted a home and a family. Commitment. And he had no doubts a lucky man smarter than himself would offer her all that and more.

The thought of her in another man's bed made him furious.

Griff threw her clothes in the case and slammed down the lid.

Was it too late? Had he hurt her so much she wouldn't give him another chance?''

Griff heard his father's voice repeating his oft-spoken phrase. *Can't know unless you try.*

What if he called and she said no?

He wouldn't call. He'd go to Seattle and see her. He could talk her into it.

Should he take Riley? He suspected she'd marry him

because she loved the baby, but he wanted her to say yes because she wanted him.

He ran down the stairs and into the kitchen, Jolie's suitcase banging against his leg.

Alice looked up, startled by his sudden entrance.

"I'm going to Seattle. Can you take care of Riley and the house for a week or so?"

She didn't even bat an eye. "I have to go to my granddaughter's dance recital on Saturday, but I can take him along."

He set the suitcase down and ran his hands through his hair. "I need a haircut. And I need to talk to the men. Pack, I have to pack."

Alice looked at him, nonplussed. "What time does your plane leave?"

Distracted, he realized she'd asked him a question. "Plane? I haven't called the airline. Wait, I'll drive her car back. Yeah, that will work."

He raced out the back door without his jacket, leaving Alice shaking her head and muttering, "About time he came to his senses."

Griff slammed into the tractor barn. Chris and Lem both leaped to their feet. "Boss, what's wrong?"

"Wrong? Nothing. I'm going to Seattle. I'm leaving you two in charge."

"When?"

"Now. Today."

Chris's face broke into a big grin. "About time."

Lem rocked back on his boot heels and nodded, his face split by a big grin.

Griff was too agitated to be annoyed with his top hands. "I'll probably be gone a week. Can you look in on Alice and Riley and take care of things around here?"

"No problem. You flying?"

"I'm going to drive Jolie's car back."

Chris, a look of longing on his face said, "Lucky. That's one fine car."

Lem rocked on his heels some more. "That's one fine woman."

All three men nodded in unison.

"Thanks. You can reach me on my cell phone if you have an emergency." He turned and walked out of the barn, leaving both his hands grinning like fools.

He wondered if they had any idea how scared he was.

Jolie stared out her bedroom window at the storm brewing over Puget Sound. When she heard a knock on her door, she glanced at her clock, surprised it was time for lunch.

"Come in."

The maid stuck her head in the room. "Miss Jolie, there's a man downstairs to see you."

She wasn't expecting anyone. "Who is it, Nadia?"

"I didn't get his name, miss. He brought your car."

"Thank you." She'd have to go down and sign for the delivery.

The final link with Griff and Riley and Montana had been delivered to her front door. She had toyed with the idea of flying back herself to get it, but driving would have been difficult. She still had the cast on her wrist.

She stood and smoothed the wrinkles out of her slacks. "Tell him I'll be right down."

Maybe it was for the best. With that last link severed maybe she could start to forget how she had fallen in love in Montana.

She came down the stairs. The foyer appeared to be empty. Perhaps Nadia had taken the man to the kitchen for something to drink.

As she got to the last step, she saw movement out of the corner of her eye. She turned, and there he was, not ten feet away.

Griff.

She froze on the step, wondering for a giddy moment if he were real. He had on dark slacks and a blue dress shirt. She'd never seen him in anything but jeans and flannel shirts.

"Hello, Jolie." His voice was quiet, his expression subdued.

Oh, God, she thought, frozen in place. Fear choked her throat. "Has something happened to Riley?"

He shook his head and took a step toward her. "No. He's fine."

She waited for him to say more, but he just stood there, staring at her, making her tremble with wanting him. "Why are you here?"

"I brought your car." He waved his hand in the direction of the front door.

That still didn't answer her question. Her father had arranged to have the car shipped. "But why are *you* here?"

"Because I didn't get a chance to say goodbye."

He hadn't called or written. In four weeks and three days she hadn't heard a word from him. "You drove all the way here to say goodbye?"

Finally he smiled. "And to thank you for everything."

"You're welcome," she said, sounding normal in spite of the fact her heart was breaking all over again.

"And to ask you to come back to Montana." He stopped in front of her and took her hands to draw her off the bottom step, frowning down at the cast on her wrist.

The feel of his hands holding hers stole her breath. It

took a moment for his words to sink in. "Isn't Alice working out?"

He ran his hands up her arms. "She's great. I don't need a nanny."

"Griff, I—"

He cut her off. "Let me say this while I can. I'm not very good with words."

Jolie looked up at his troubled face, afraid of what he was going to say.

"I thought I'd never have feelings for anyone again. It hurt too much." He let go of her hand and made a fist over his heart. "Here. But when you left, I realized how much I had come to care for you."

"What do you want from me?" Jolie held her breath.

He brought their clasped hands to his lips. "I love you. Jolie, will you marry me?"

Stunned, she stood staring up at him. "What?"

He dropped her hand and pulled her into his arms. He lowered his face to hers and brushed his lips across her mouth.

In a low tone he said, "You heard me. I love you. I want to get married."

She began to tremble in his arms. "When?" If this was all a dream she never wanted to wake up.

He picked her up and spun her around. "Today. Right now!"

She threw her arms around his neck, tears running down her cheeks. "Oh, Griff, I've missed you so much. And Riley."

He laughed. "Good. Because he's part of the package."

Face solemn, she wiggled out of his grasp and held him at arm's length. "I want more children." Jolie studied his face.

"Sure. We can manage that. Want to start right now?" He wiggled his eyebrows at her.

Jolie threw herself back into his arms. "I love you so much."

Griff kissed her again, then pushed her back far enough that she could see his face. "You didn't answer my question."

At her puzzled look he said, "Say yes!"

"Yes, yes, yes!"

He laughed and hauled her into his warm embrace. "I will love you, Jolie Carleton, for the rest of my life."

"Good. Because I'm never letting you go." She knew she had the courage to hold on to what she loved most.

Forever.

*   *   *   *   *

Start Your Summer With Sizzle
And Silhouette Books!

In June 2002, look for these HOT volumes led by
New York Times bestselling authors and
receive a free Gourmet Garden kit!

Retail value of $17.00 U.S.

THE BLUEST EYES IN TEXAS by Joan Johnston
and WIFE IN NAME ONLY by Carolyn Zane

THE LEOPARD'S WOMAN by Linda Lael Miller
and WHITE WOLF by Lindsay McKenna

THE BOUNTY by Rebecca Brandewyne
and A LITTLE TEXAS TWO-STEP by Peggy Moreland

OVERLOAD by Linda Howard
and IF A MAN ANSWERS by Merline Lovelace

**This exciting promotion is available at your
favorite retail outlet. See inside books for details.**

Only from

Silhouette®
Where love comes alive™

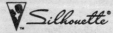

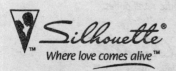